GOLDEN ISLAND

Translated by Edelgard von Heydekampf Bruehl

Illustrated by John Kaufmann

DOUBLEDAY & COMPANY, INC., GARDEN CITY, NEW YORK

Golden Island

By KATHERINE ALLFREY

1

The island was small and lay far away from the world in the deep blue, ever restless sea. It was such an insignificant island that the big steamboat from Piraeus did not even stop at it but instead went on to the large neighboring island and unloaded everything there: the mail and a little cargo, somebody returning from a trip, or one of its rare visitors. It was even more unusual for tradespeople to come to the island. Tourists never did. The island was too remote, too poor and stony, and there was nothing to admire, neither slim white columns nor ancient Cyclopean walls.

Yet the island was beautiful like all the other small islands in the Aegean Sea. Its inhabitants even felt that it was the most beautiful one of all and called it Kalonysos, which means Beautiful Island. The rock on its western side rose straight out of the sea like a horn and was covered by a close-set mosaic of white houses. This was the Chora, the first settlement and for many years the only one on the island. In the center was the church with its bell tower. The Chora was still regarded as the capital even though the harbor town on the east coast had long since surpassed it in importance.

Here life went on in its old way in the narrow alleys which were steep at the beginning, became steeper —still steeper—pushing on up with one, two steps and finally ending in narrow stairs. Up here the houses no longer had yards, only nooks and corners, and everything—alleys, steps, nooks, houses—all were a snowy white.

Most of the houses were small white rectangles or cubes set helter-skelter, without rhyme or reason, on top, underneath or alongside one another. The village had not been planned; it had grown, and the rock had dictated its form. If the people had had any plan at all it was to live close together, to climb as high as possible and to leave the water far below. For the water around the island, so blue and shimmering, was yet wide and open and full of danger. This was the sea over which the pirates had come to burn and loot and kill when the Chora was being settled. The Chora had had to be a fort where the people could find protection. It was only later, when times grew calmer and the Corsairs disappeared from the sea, that once in a while someone dared to build down below, near the bay where there was more room and even some land for gardening. And so it had remained. Most of the people preferred to live high up and close together.

In front of the last of the houses at the shore sat a girl. Her name was Andrula. She lived here with her mother. They were the smallest family in the smallest

house in the village. In fact you could not even call it a family for there was no longer a father. Andreas, who had built the house for himself and his young bride, Evangelia, had gone out to sea sponge-fishing soon after the wedding and had never come back. The sea had kept him. That is why Evangelia and Andrula were so poor. The young mother had put on black clothes and had never since dressed in anything but black.

Yet their home was beautiful despite their poverty. The house consisted of only one room, but the room opened onto a small yard and that is where they actually lived. Andreas had planted a grapevine close to the door and it had grown so tall that its branches had long since covered the whole yard. The leaves were soft and shiny in the spring when the sunlight was no more than a gentle smile, and thick and protective during the summer when it stabbed like a sword at everyone who walked out from their shelter. Heavy grapes hung in clusters in late summer, pale green and dull gold, close to each other. They were beauty and wealth at the same time.

There were also several fig trees near the house. Two of them bore small, wild purple figs, but the third and biggest one bore cultivated fruit, big as pears with rose-red meat, sweet as honey. Andrula's mother sold the beautiful figs, but they could eat as much as they wanted of the little wild ones, and these too were sweet. Every year they dried many of them, strung them on reeds and hung them like wreaths on the walls of their room. This way they had something sweet to eat during the winter. Oranges and lemons would not grow on the island. They had to be brought in from more fertile coasts and paid for with money. But money was such a rarity to Evangelia that she used it with the utmost care and only for the dire necessities: for oil and flour and beans, for shoes, for charcoal on which to cook, and for the kerosene which gave them light.

As soon as the winter passed and the weather turned fair and dependable, Evangelia brought her weaving loom outside and put it under the budding grapevine. Then she took a deep breath and looked around as she pushed her seat into place. She could see the sea from here, a part of the Chora and the path which ran inland from the shore. The whole summer long she and An-drula lived in the open air, and when the time of the great heat came they even slept outside, sheltered by the great vine.

This time had now come. The grapes were beginning to ripen. One could almost see them soaking up the sun and turning it into sweetness. Every day Andrula looked longingly up at them. She could hardly wait until they were ripe. But she had to have patience. Her mother still said no: "Not yet! Maybe tomorrow."

2

Andrula walked across the sun-parched field, pulled down by the earthen water jug she carried. It was heavy and its reddish clay shimmered with moisture. She had fetched cool, fresh drinking water from a well farther inland. They had their own well in the yard but being so close to the sea the water was brackish and only good for washing and cleaning.

Andrula stepped through the small gate and carefully put the crock in the deepest shade where every possible breeze would reach it. This way the evaporation in the porous jug kept the water sweet and cool.

Evangelia smiled at her. The clatter of the loom was not interrupted for even a moment. It continued evenly through the whole long day—the soft squeaking sound of the harness' rise and fall, the wide throw of the shuttle from one hand to the other and the hard clap as the thread was pushed firmly into place. Hour after hour, and very fast: squeak—hush—clap, squeak—hush —clap, squeak—hush—clap. Andrula had grown up with this sound. She noticed it no more than she heard the soft chatter of the waves lapping the nearby beach.

"Manula," said Andrula, pushing her heavy black hair out of her eyes. "May I go into the village now? To play?"

"Yes, run along," said Evangelia, sighing softly. She would have liked it better if Andrula had stayed with her as she did when she was still small. But she was growing up. She went to school now and she wanted to be with children her own age. It was a pity there were no children in the neighborhood who could come over to play. Then Andrula would not always want to run off.

"Yes, run along," Evangelia repeated. She found it hard to refuse her daughter anything. "But be back at midday."

More than once Andrula had shared a meal wherever she was playing at the time. This was not unusual in the Chora. Weren't they all one big family? But Evangelia did not approve of that. Her child belonged at her own table, and as long as she was able to earn the money for a soup, Andrula should not eat at other tables. Andrula thought differently, or rather she did not think at all, but accepted freely what was offered to her.

She ran happily up the hill on the other side of the road to get to the village as quickly as possible. She could hear her friends from a distance. They were at the lower square singing loudly:

"You go by, Kyra Maria,
You go by, you go by!"

Andrula could hear clearly the voice of her cousin
Stassa, who sang shriller than the others and always
a little off key.

Now Andrula joined them and she and Stassa, the
tallest ones, formed an arch with their arms and hands
and a chain of little children filed through:

"Look, here comes the honey bee
With her children, one, two, three."

Andrula thought of herself as the leader of the group
since she was the oldest, the tallest, and also the most
inventive of them all. But Stassa saw herself as the
leader because she had three big brothers and because
her father owned one of the two taverns in the village.
She wore better and more beautiful dresses and white
sandals, while Andrula walked barefoot in the summer.
For days at a time they would play peacefully together
but suddenly, completely unexpectedly, something would
come over Stassa. She had to bring Andrula down a peg,
no matter how. As far down as possible—where she
belonged.

This bad spirit stirred in Stassa when she heard her
rival say before the beginning of the next game: "Now
I am king, and you—"

"Why should you be king?" Stassa shouted. "You, of
all people! You are nothing but a beggar child!"

Andrula flared up. "I never begged for anything in
my life! I am not a beggar child!"

"You are," jeered Stassa. "My mother said if we didn't feed you once in a while you wouldn't have a bit of flesh on your bones!"

Andrula stood stunned. Her face was so furious that Stassa retreated a step. But still she went on:

"And she wants to be king—in that shabby dress! Look at her. She has nothing to wear but what her mother keeps from other people's bedclothes!"

That was too much for Andrula to take. She screamed and flew at her enemy. The next moment they were tearing each other's hair. The younger children drew away. A couple of women hurried up to separate the little fighting cats.

"What a way to behave!" they scolded. "Are you girls or animals? Go! Go on home if you can't play nicely together." They shook them hard and pushed each one on her way.

Stassa ran home screaming to tell her mother. Andrula ran off too, but not screaming and not home. Things like this she could not tell her mother, these horrible things Stassa had said! Anyway, her mother must not see her like this, torn and scratched and beside herself with rage.

She turned off shortly before the last houses and climbed down a small, narrow path to the shore. Down here there was nobody except the fisherman Sotiris' wife, who was washing her mats. She didn't even look up and Andrula slipped quickly past her.

Behind this cove, which was called the Great Sand, there was another smaller one on the other side of a tiny hidden inlet among the rocks. The coast was very steep at this point and the water was deep. Andrula was strictly forbidden to come here. But she knew that the people of the village hardly ever came this way; they had no reason to, and that was why the little cove was such a good refuge.

She had to climb over broad stones, around stiff and prickly bushes, between and under the branches of a pine tree which had fallen a long time ago. On the shore were giant gray and brown rocks. One was big and smooth like a table; the waves washed over its top. Next to it two or three rocks formed a trough in which the water was like a mirror. Andrula knelt down and looked into it.

What a sight she was! Hair all tousled, two long scratches on her left cheek, her face tear-stained. That Stassa! I should have pulled out every hair on her head, thought Andrula, full of anger, as she dipped the hem of her skirt into the sun-warmed water to wash her face. How it stung!

Andrula let herself fall onto the next dry rock. All of a sudden she was very tired. Stassa had hurt her terribly with her wicked and poisonous tongue. But wasn't it the truth? This dress really *was* woven of yarn left over from one of her mother's orders. It was the custom: what was left over and not enough for another piece belonged to the weaver. It was part of her payment. Everyone knew that.

But Stassa had not meant it that way. She meant that her mother had used someone else's yarn for herself.

Andrula leaned her small defiant chin in both hands and stared out over the shimmering sea. Under the damp strands of hair her forehead was still troubled, but now more from hurt than from anger.

If I had a father or a brother, she reflected, then nobody would dare say a thing like that to me. Then my mother wouldn't have to work at the loom. And I

would even have a white dress with lots of little
flowers on it, made of cloth bought at the store. Stassa
had that kind of dress, she even had two, but the other
one was green with white stars.

A great sadness came over Andrula. She sat for a
long time on her rock and looked out over the sea at
the pure blue which rose and fell, sending clear waves
onto the shore. Not far from her, two brownish cones
rose from the water, a larger one and a smaller one.
These were the islands of Ryos and Anti-Ryos. Andrula
could see them from her house, too. But now as the
sun was about to set, letting all colors stand out more
vividly, a third island appeared between the two, far
away on the horizon. First it shimmered golden, then
faded to a deep rose. How beautiful! It seemed to float
above the water.

Andrula looked at it a long time.

But suddenly she started. It must be late if the sun
painted the world with these colors. Quickly she
clambered over the rocky crevice and ran home as fast
as her feet would carry her. Now she realized, too, how
very hungry she was.

3

There had been angry words at home, and as punishment Andrula was not permitted to go to the village to play the next day. Not that she cared. She did not want to have anything to do with the other children. Let Stassa be the king. It was Andrula's game, so they would not get very far with it. She was the only one who knew it because she had invented it. Besides, today she was not king but shipbuilder. She had found a piece of driftwood shaped almost like a sailboat. All it needed was a mast.

Andrula tinkered with her boat and managed to insert a thin stick as a mast. She begged a piece of white cloth from her mother, cut a sail from it and fastened the little triangle to the stick with infinite care. Now anyone could see that it was a sailboat. She was happy and proud and her mother had to write *Agios Andreas* on the bow with a piece of charcoal because she could do it better than Andrula. *Agios Andreas* was to be the name of the boat, after her patron saint.

Evangelia was glad to see her little girl so content

and busy at her side. If only it could always be that way! Maybe it would be, from now on. Andrula was growing up. It wouldn't be long before the wild little girl changed into an obedient, understanding daughter. And so the next morning, when Andrula wanted to go down to the water and sail her boat, Evangelia permitted it at once.

Andrula ran off happily, the small boat under her arm. The fight in the village had been forgotten. It did not mean anything anymore. Her own creation, her boat and playing with it was now the only thing in her mind.

But Stassa was on the beach and she had not forgotten so quickly. She gathered her crowd of playmates behind her like a sheepdog with his herd and declared with hostility, "We're not playing with you anymore."

And the others repeated the words after her. Even the smallest one cried, "We're not playing with you anymore!"

Andrula turned her back on them. But Stassa's curiosity was stronger than her hostility.

"What have you got there?" she wanted to know.

"My sailboat," said Andrula, who could not suppress her pride. "I'm going down to sail it now."

"Oh, aren't you ashamed of yourself?" called Stassa, indignantly. "Look at her. There she goes—over where the big boys swim!" And all her followers shouted, "Shame on you, shame on you!" after Andrula.

But they did not bother Andrula. Let them shout! She had her boat, and she had seen only too clearly the envy in Stassa's eyes. She ignored them and ran straight down to the water. Carefully she put the *Agios Andreas* into the wet sand, stuffed her clean skirt into the shorts she wore underneath, and waded into the water with her boat.

This was the place where a group of bigger boys played every morning with their boats made of wood or tin. It was a wild and noisy game, because they fought real sea battles. They were Turks and Fighters for Freedom. Everyone was an admiral, and each of the battered, weatherbeaten craft represented a whole fleet. Or sometimes they played smugglers and police, which was just as exciting.

Most of the time they were much too preoccupied to pay any attention even to smaller boys, let alone girls. But a girl going into the water to sail anything like a boat—that was unheard of. That was not to be tolerated.

"Hey, little one," called Spiros, the biggest of the boys. "What are you doing there?" He plowed through the water toward Andrula, and the others followed him, pulling their boats.

"I am sailing my boat," answered Andrula. She tried to keep her little vessel straight, but it was always falling on its side because it had no keel.

"Boat?" jeered Spiros, coming closer quickly. "Just who do you think you are? One of us?"

He fished the poor little thing out of the water and looked it over. Then he laughed loudly and shouted, "Boat, she says. Is this supposed to be a boat? It's nothing

but a piece of driftwood!" He gripped it at both ends—

"No, don't!" shouted Andrula, pleading. But too late. It crunched—cracked—and was broken in two.

Contemptuously the boy threw the pieces way out into the sea.

"There," he said. "Now go home and play with your doll." Having laid down the law, he felt like quite a hero. He returned to his friends, leaving Andrula standing there.

She could just see the broken pieces of her *Agios Andreas* as they were lifted by the next small wave and drifted toward her. With a sob she turned around and splashed back to the beach. Blinded by tears, she ran home. This was a misery she did not have to hide. She stumbled into the yard and buried her face in her mother's black dress.

"Hush, hush," murmured Evangelia soothingly. "Hush, my little bird, my tiny one. What happened?"

"My boat," sobbed Andrula. "My beautiful boat!"

"Hush, hush," whispered Evangelia, rocking her to and fro gently in her arms. But Andrula was inconsolable and only sobbed louder, until anger flared up in her, and with it the desire for revenge.

"Aren't you going to tell his father, Manula, that Spiros is cruel and that he broke my boat?"

"I can't do that," answered Evangelia as she tried to free herself from the clutching arms. "We want to live in peace with our neighbors."

Andrula raised her tear-stained face and looked incredulously at her mother. "No? You mean you are not going to tell Spiros' father? But he ruined my boat!"

Evangelia threw the shuttle through the taut-strung threads. "It was really only a piece of driftwood," she murmured.

Andrula did not say anything. She looked at her mother, unable to comprehend. Stassa had rejected her, Spiros had chased her away, and now her mother, too, was deserting her. "Only a piece of driftwood," she had said, just like that thief down at the beach, that Spiros.

Andrula walked over to the water jug near the wall. There she washed her burning face over the earthen bowl. Then she went out the gate and sat down in her favorite place, underneath the window. But she did not look out at the sea or over toward the Chora. She sat motionless, staring at her feet. She was more lonely than she had ever been in her life. Maybe she would always be as lonely as this, if even her own mother took sides against her!

"And it was not just a piece of driftwood," she suddenly said out loud. "It was a boat, brand-new. Freshly painted like ivory, with a yellow, a blue, and a brown line all around it. And the new sail was white—white as snow."

She raised her eyes and could see her proud, strong boat in the quiet bay. It swayed gently and it turned

slowly, almost unnoticeably, around its anchor chain. Now she stood on deck, and now she sailed off, her little dinghy in tow.

She sailed far, far away from her homeland and Stassa, far away from Spiros and his gang, far away, too, from the little house, toward other islands, great, beautiful, and rich with wells, islands like gardens. Yes, the gardens grew all the way down to the sea.

Behind her, through the clatter of the loom, she could hear her mother singing. Evangelia always did that when she was troubled or worried. She had a clear, low voice, and she was singing the song, "Oh My Sea."

Andrula hummed softly, and by the time the song ended she had at least forgiven her mother.

She went in obediently when she was called to the table, though she was quieter than usual. She did not have much appetite, and she answered her mother's concerned question about it by saying it was too hot to eat. She slept through most of the afternoon, and in the evening she again sat beneath the window. What else was there to do but stare over toward Ryos and Anti-Ryos.

Suddenly Andrula sat up straight. Sure enough, the third island, the far one, she could see it from here! Of course it was only a tiny tip of it, because Ryos pushed out her long hill in front of it, but it was there, there was no doubt about it. All golden! And now once again it changed to rose, now to violet, and the sun went down. The world was gray and blue, and suddenly it was night.

Andrula decided she would sit here every evening at sunset. But she sighed. Life used to be more fun.

4

All the next day Andrula was very quiet. She did little chores for her mother, swept the room and the yard and sprinkled the floor with water to bring a little coolness to the burning hours of the day. For the heat was great, and it was getting still hotter.

Later Andrula cut up tomatoes, peppers, and onions for a salad, took goat's cheese from the screened cupboard and bread from the breadbox, and it was still half an hour until lunch. But there was nothing else for her to do. So they ate half an hour earlier than usual, and that made the afternoon even longer.

Evangelia could hardly recognize this good little daughter. Just a short time ago she had been wishing for just such a child, quiet, helpful, and close to her. But Andrula was so joyless. There she sat in her corner again, drawing crosses and circles in the sand with her toe, not saying a word. Her mother sighed. If only school would start again! But that was a long time off.

Toward evening, when it cooled off a little, she asked,

"Don't you want to go to the village and play with the other children?"

"I'll never go there again," answered Andrula.

"Oh, don't say that. You have been home all day."

"No," said Andrula. She drew some water from the well and began to water the flower pots.

Her mother went on working quietly for a little while, then looked at Andrula again. "Do you feel sick?" she asked.

"No," replied Andrula.

"I have a job for you," said Evangelia. "But if you don't feel well, or are too tired, you don't have to do it."

"What kind of a job?" Andrula wanted to know, curious now.

"Poor Katsika," said Evangelia, motioning with her head toward the old goat that was looking over the wall. "She must be awfully tired of picking at the same bushes all the time. And because you are a big girl now and help me with so many chores, perhaps you would like to take Katsika across the fields so she can find some other food."

"But I won't go over that way," warned Andrula, pointing toward the houses in the village.

"No, of course not," said her mother soothingly. "What would Katsika find there? Here on our side, and farther over, on the hills, there is a lot for her to pick. I would pack a lunch for you, just like a real goatherd."

Early the next morning Evangelia put bread and

cheese into a brightly striped satchel, cut off the first bunch of grapes and put it on top.

"Take the little jug with you so you'll have something to drink," she said. Andrula filled the little jug from the big one and closed it with a pine cone wrapped in a clean piece of cloth. Equipped like this, she could stay out until evening.

"God go with you," said her mother lovingly. "And come home before dark."

The goat did not have to be led. She followed like a dog. But when they took the path across the fields she began to find this to sniff and that to nibble, here a half-withered shrub, there a prickly creeper, and over there a gray-green leaf, so that she pushed on ahead, wanting to be everywhere at once. The unaccustomed freedom made her skittish and she almost trotted along, neck stretched out and udder swinging.

Andrula's spirits rose too. "Isn't this better, Katsika, than being home on a rope?" she cried, and she reached playfully for the goat's curved horns. She found a stick and swung it through the air. She was not a little girl with just one goat, but a goatherd with a large flock, and her old Katsika was the leader. So many goats followed her that the fields were filled with the high and low sounds of their bells.

It took them quite a while to come to the place where Andrula planned to stop for lunch and rest during the hot noon hours. She had made a wide detour, be-

cause Katsika was forever finding a new bush which she had to sample. Being a goatherd was fun, but it was also tiring. Finally they reached the narrow rill which led down to the sea, to the little cove. Some scrub cast a thin shadow. It would have to do as a stopping place.

With a sigh of relief Andrula let the colored satchel slide from her shoulder. She rubbed the red line where the cord had dug into her skin. She put the little jug down with great care. If it should spill she would have to remain thirsty. There was neither spring nor well in this area.

She broke her bread and began to eat. The goat came closer, curious, and Andrula gave her a little piece of the crust. "There, that's for you. But you have been eating all morning long!" The goat bleated softly—it

sounded like laughter—then began looking for herbs between the rocks, for thyme and marjoram and anything
that would taste fragrant and spicy.

The goat's cheese was sharp, too, and very salty. Andrula ate it, finished her bread, and followed it up with
a couple of grapes from her large cluster. The first grape
of the year! The first one and the best one. Tomorrow
or the day after tomorrow they might be sweeter, but
this first grape was the best of all. Andrula closed her
eyes and savored it as the smooth little ball burst in
her mouth and filled it with coolness. And then it ran
sweet and fresh down her throat. Nothing was so re-
freshing! Not even water.

But just because these were the first grapes of this
summer, she must not eat them too quickly. The day
ahead was still long. Now she was ready to drink some
water and then sleep, as all goatherds did. She looked
for the spot under her bush where the shade was dens-
est, and left the jug and the cluster of grapes under its
protection. Then she rolled up the satchel, which was
to be her pillow. She looked around once again for
Katsika, who had lain down near a large rock and
seemed to think that she was in the shade too. Then
Andrula lay down, put her tousled dark head down on
the satchel, and immediately fell asleep.

It must have been about two hours later when a
light breeze came in from the sea and woke the little
goatherd. She sat up, yawned widely and rubbed her
eyes.

She had slept very soundly, and now she was

thirsty. The water in the jug was still cool, and she still had almost the whole cluster of grapes left. She knew where she was going to eat them—down below, on the flat rock where the water could wash over her feet. There she would sit and eat her grapes. And she would see the far island light up, just as it had that first evening.

Old Katsika came along as she started to go. But she so much preferred the stony slope, with all its different kinds of scrubby bushes, that she soon stayed behind.

Andrula sat all alone on the smooth flat rock, the grapes in her hand.

5

Ryos and Anti-Ryos were still wearing their daytime colors, brownish at the bottom and gray-green at the top, so it couldn't be very late. The third, the far island, could not be seen, only sensed. The waves rolled sleepily into the cove. The water slapped softly against the sun-heated stones and washed again and again over Andrula's dusty feet on the ledge. Nothing else was moving. It was completely still.

Andrula began to realize what a long time she had been alone today. Tending Katsika on the way, she had not felt it so much. She had played goatherd and the hours had passed quickly. But now she wished she had one of her friends with her. Not Stassa. Stassa was her enemy. But maybe Klio, or Marigo—someone with whom she could share the grapes, someone she could talk to.

Far out in the sea something stirred. Andrula sat up straight. Dolphins! She forgot her grapes and her loneliness because already two, three smooth, shining bodies rose from the waves, did a half turn effortlessly in the air and dived into the water again. There were at least

six of these beautiful animals. They leaped in pairs.
Sometimes four of them were in the air at once.

Were they playing together? They looked as if they
were having such fun. Andrula had never seen so many
dolphins at one time before. She watched the big fish,
spellbound, and not without envy as they went by dancing and leaping. How she wished she could join them!
But . . . "Are they something to be afraid of?" she said
under her breath.

"Nonsense." A soft, strangely whistling but completely intelligible voice came to her from the water.
"No one need be afraid of us."

Andrula started. She looked around, naturally in the
direction of the land. But she did not see a soul anywhere.

"Are you looking for me on the land, silly?" It whistled again, and this time it sounded amused. "Look toward the water!"

And sure enough, there in front of her, close by,
swam a dolphin who could talk. For there was nobody
else nearby who could have spoken. She examined him
more closely—the peculiarly pointed snout, the beautifully rounded forehead, two intelligent eyes which bore
no resemblance to fish eyes at all and which looked longingly at the bunch of grapes in her hand.

"Little girl," he began for a third time, "little girl,
stop dreaming! And please give me one of your grapes."

Andrula shook herself like a puppy that has just
come out of the water. Surely she was awake. She was

completely awake. She was sitting in the little cove on her rock, and before her was a dolphin who could speak and who wanted her grapes. Suddenly she laughed aloud and lifted up the bunch, ready to throw it to him.

"Slowly, slowly!" he said with his whistling voice. "One grape for you, one for me, all right? Then we can enjoy them much longer."

Andrula nodded eagerly. She carefully chose the biggest, most beautiful grape. "Catch!" she cried, and she let the grape fly high through the air. Before it could reach the water the big fish leaped toward it and caught it with a most graceful turn.

"Bravo, bravo!" cried Andrula. "You did that beautifully!"

The dolphin could even smile, and if he had had a hand he would certainly have put it on his chest and thanked her politely as all the children of the Chora had been taught to do.

Now Andrula ate a grape too, but that was only a formality. Then she threw another one to the dolphin, and another and still another. He caught each one easily, even when she began to throw them in different directions. He was incredibly quick and agile. Andrula laughed out loud.

Suddenly a thought struck her. She hesitated, looking from the remaining grapes in her left hand to her new playmate and back again to the fragile stems, now almost bare.

For a change the dolphin performed some diving

tricks. He turned as smoothly as an eel, and then he
came closer again.

"Oh, are they all gone?" he asked. "Or is it your turn
now?"

Andrula shook her head. "Do dolphins really eat
grapes?" she asked slowly.

"Most of them don't," explained the dolphin readily.
"But I have always had a particular liking for grapes.
Tell me, did you get your share? When it comes to
grapes, I am greedy."

"We have many at home," said Andrula. "Come back
tomorrow and I'll bring you a much more beautiful
bunch."

"Oh please do!" said the dolphin. "I'll be looking forward to tomorrow."

"Me too," cried Andrula, and she waved after him as

he swam off, showing her some of his most beautiful leaps.

The two islands had turned the color of violets, and between them rose the far one, the third island, in shining gold. Andrula sat and gazed over at it dreamily. Was that where her dolphin was going?

At that moment she heard the pitiful bleating of poor Katsika, and it brought her quickly back to earth. She climbed up as fast as she could and led the goat home by the shortest route.

"How late you are!" called her mother, who was standing at the gate looking for her. "There was no need to stay out so long! Where have you been the whole day?"

"In the fields. Katsika liked it there," answered the child.

"I'm sure she did. But you have probably had enough

of herding after such a long day in the fields, and all
by yourself," said Evangelia.

"No, I liked it there too," said Andrula. She filled a
beaker with water, drank thirstily, and filled it once
more. Then she looked up at the grapes which hung
full right above her, and she smiled a secret smile.

"Tomorrow I'll go out again," she announced.

"What did you say?" asked her mother, who was going
back and forth as she brought a plate of fried potatoes,
a tomato salad, and some goat's cheese to the table. She
cut large pieces of the dark bread. "Tomorrow you run
along and play in the village, like the other children."

"I'll never play with them again," murmured Andrula,
and she reached for the potatoes. Her mother milked
the goat quickly, and then she too sat down. Above
them in the leaves swung the old kerosene lamp.

Andrula realized now how very hungry she was. She
ate her piece of cheese and asked for a second one and
she finished almost all of the tomato salad. How good
the bread tasted! It was fresh; her mother had baked it
today.

"May I have some grapes, Manula?" she asked.

"I will see whether there are any more ripe ones,"
said Evangelia. She climbed onto her chair and looked
around carefully. "Here, this one should be sweet
enough," she said, cutting down a small but heavy
bunch.

"Thank you very much, Manula," murmured Andrula politely. She plucked a grape, threw it into the
air, and tried to catch it with her lips. But no matter

how wide she opened her mouth, the grape hit her chin and rolled to the floor. She tried it again, and again she failed. The second grape, too, rolled onto the floor.

"What are you doing?" her mother cried, really angry "I have not had a single grape yet and you are throwing them around. Aren't you ashamed, treating beautiful grapes like that!"

Andrula was sorry, but she had only wanted to find out if she could do it too, catch grapes like the dolphin. He even did it while he swam. She was very proud of him. It was too bad she could not tell her mother. She would never believe it. Sweet and kind as her mother was, she was, after all, a grown-up. One could not talk with grown-ups about everything, even though one wanted to sometimes.

So she just said, "I am sorry, Manula," and was as good as gold for the rest of the evening. She washed the two plates and the two forks and the knife which they had shared, and put everything away. Then she helped to roll out the bedding and put the pillows in place.

She was almost too tired to wash her feet, but her mother insisted. Finally Evangelia blew out the lamp and lay down next to Andrula on the large mat.

"Good night," murmured Andrula sleepily.

Whispering softly, the waves rolled onto the beach. Evangelia listened to them for a long time.

6

The next day Evangelia would not let Andrula out of her sight. Again and again she found something else for her daughter to do—carry water, sweep the floor, sort white beans for soup—she even sent her to the store for red thread. This was one order Andrula did not like to carry out. First, she did not like to go up to the Chora —and where else could you find red thread?—and second, the walk into the village and back took much too much time. It was so late already! She ran the whole way, came home overheated, and was scolded into the bargain.

It was really not late at all. In her impatience she had gotten up an hour earlier than usual, and her small tasks had not taken even half the time she thought they had. In the end she was on her way to the fields at almost the same time as yesterday.

Katsika was just as impatient as Andrula, and could not wait to get to the fields. She bleated loudly and happily, eager to push on. But when they came to the place where the little shrubs and bushes grew, and the goat set out to savor everything in a leisurely manner, Andrula did not let her have her way. She pressed on without stopping until they reached the place above the cove. The poor old goat was almost too tired to feed. She only looked for a spot of shade, and found it in front of a rock.

"Yes, you stay there," said Andrula, feeling sorry for her now. "I'll run down quickly. I'll be right back." She could not wait to see the dolphin.

But the little cove was empty. And the sea, so big, so lovely, was empty too. Nothing stirred anywhere. Nowhere even the ripple of a wave. Neither in the distance nor close by were any smooth, shining shapes rising from the waves and leaping over them.

Deeply disappointed, Andrula turned around and clambered back up the cliff. He had not come! And he had promised! He had even said he was looking forward to it. And she had such nice grapes for him. She had wanted to give him all her grapes, because he liked them so much. She felt like throwing the grapes away, now.

Then she remembered that they had not set a time to meet. She was simply too early. Yesterday she had slept later, and had been much later going down to the water. And even though she had not been early getting away from home today, she had hurried so much on the way that she had more than made up for lost time. How she had hurried that poor Katsika! She felt so relieved that she was able to be truly sorry, and she promised to give her at least half of her bread, maybe even more.

The goat was still in her little shady spot when Andrula returned, and the girl put her arms around her neck tenderly. "You do like to go grazing with me, don't you, Katsika? And you'll be good and eat, won't you? There are so many bushes here. And look, my bread— it's for you. But don't run away! I have to go down to the rock, and there is nothing down there for you. You just stay here until I come back."

This time the big fish was swimming around in the cove near the rocks when Andrula jumped onto the flat stone, the cluster of grapes in her hand. He had already seen her and quickly swam nearer.

"You kept your word!" he greeted her, gurgling softly, as if laughing deep in his throat.

"Of course, and you did too," rejoiced Andrula. "Catch!" And they played the grape game until even the last and smallest one had disappeared into his mouth.

"It seems to me that I always get your share too," he said, and if he were trying to sound ashamed or sorry, he did not succeed. On the contrary, he seemed rather happy about it.

"Yes," admitted Andrula, laughing. "But you do like grapes so much, don't you? And you probably don't get them very often."

"Never," said the dolphin. "Never, since that time."

"When was 'that time'?" asked Andrula curiously.

"In the old days," he answered. He swam back and forth slowly and began to speak.

"Once, a long, long time ago," he began, "a ship sailed across this sea, not far from here. It was manned with dark, wild fellows, but its passenger was fair, young, and handsome. This woke evil thoughts in the sailors, and they began to look at him secretly. They whispered among themselves: 'How would it be if we attacked him and tied him up? Such a strong young man would bring a lot of money on the slave market. Or we could hold him captive and ask a high ransom.'

"The plan seemed a good one, and so easy to carry out. Weren't there many of them against one man? But this one . . .

"He sat quietly in the bow of the ship, looked at them and laughed. Suddenly one of the villains screamed and pointed with trembling finger at the mast and at the spars, and when the others looked they screamed too, or were stunned into silence. For from the mast, from the rowing benches, from all the woodwork of the ship, stems were sprouting, buds were breaking and shoots climbing upward. Ivy and grapevines were reaching this way and that, all at once bearing leaves and blossoms and ripe fruit. And all around the ship could be heard the music of flutes and the singing of nightingales, and there was the scent of wine. Where the stranger had been sitting there now stood a lion, a huge golden beast. He raised his head and roared.

"The sailors were gripped by such fear that they

threw themselves into the sea, all of them except the helmsman. He had not joined in the plot."

"Why not?" whispered Andrula tensely.

"Because he must have sensed who it was that was sailing with them."

"And who was it?"

"A god," said the dolphin. "A new and mighty god."

Andrula did not know quite what to make of a god. She was content to leave him under his vines and grapes and concern herself with matters closer at hand. "And the sailors?" she asked.

"They were turned into dolphins as soon as they hit the water."

"Oh-h," marveled Andrula, and she thought for a while. "Were you one of them?" she asked with the most innocent face in the world.

"Ask me no questions and I'll tell you no lies," the dolphin retorted quickly.

"No, please, just a moment!" urged Andrula. "The ship with the golden lion and the grapes—what happened to the ship?"

"It sailed on like a garden in bloom. And the lion changed back into the fair young man. He plucked the grapes from the mast and from the spars and threw them overboard, right and left, to the dolphins. And he laughed as they leaped for them."

"He laughed," repeated Andrula dreamily. She saw everything: the green-leafed ship, the heavy bunches of grapes, pale golden, reddish and dark blue. "How beautiful! What a lovely story! Do you know another one?"

"Many," answered the dolphin. "But it is better to live them than to listen to them. Would you like to live the next story?"

"Yes," cried Andrula eagerly. "Yes!"

"Not far from here," he began, "there is an island—"

"Do you mean the third one, the golden island which can only be seen at sunset?" Andrula interrupted him.

"Yes, I mean that one. Do you know it?"

"No, I have never been away from Kalonysos. But I would love to go there some day."

"Why not?" remarked the dolphin as if it were the simplest thing in the world.

"Why not?" repeated Andrula. "How would I get there? I can't swim like you!"

"And I can't go into the vineyards and pick grapes like you," answered the dolphin. "But we can help each other. You would like to visit the island; I will take you there."

"You will take me there?" Andrula asked doubtfully.

"Yes. On my back." He gurgled again as if something amused him. "You wouldn't be the first human being to go across the sea on a dolphin's back!"

"Could you really? Now? Right away?" Andrula cried, jumping up.

"No, of course not right now, little silly. It is much too late. Look, the islands look almost dark blue."

And so they were, and the far island shimmered nearly crimson between them, far, far, far on the horizon.

Andrula jumped up.

"Tomorrow then," she called hastily. "Tomorrow morning!"

Without waiting for an answer, she climbed over the rocks up the steep cliff. She had to run after the goat, who had started home on her own.

7

Evangelia was very angry when Andrula got home at last.

"It is already dark outside," she said reproachfully. "Is it necessary to stay out so long? You always used to know when it was time to come home."

"Yes, but that was when I played with the other children, and when they went home I did too," Andrula defended herself.

"That is true," said her mother, and she added, "I wish you would play with the other children in the village. It isn't right for a little girl to spend her whole day in the fields, all alone."

"You are alone all day long too," Andrula pointed out.

"I am a grown woman and no longer a child," admonished her mother. "That is different. Tomorrow you'll be a good girl, won't you, and go and play with the other children?"

"They don't want me and I don't want them," said Andrula stubbornly. And when her mother shook her head she said, "But Katsika has to be taken to the fields!"

"She has been out enough now. It won't hurt her to stay for a while and nibble at the bushes here."

Andrula was troubled. Could this end with her mother not letting her go off on her own anymore? Not even tomorrow, when the dolphin was going to take her to the island? She began to plead, putting her arms around her mother's neck. "Oh Manula, do let me go! It is so beautiful out there on the hills. There is so much to see—falcons high up in the air and quails almost under my feet, and the day before yesterday I even saw dolphins far out in the water."

"Dolphins?" asked her mother suspiciously. "You were not down at the little cove, at the rocks?"

Andrula quickly checked herself. "No, not all the way down. You can see far out over the sea from above, and that's how I saw the dolphins." It was a lie, and she could not bring herself to look at her mother.

"Make sure that you don't go down to the bay by yourself!" ordered Evangelia sternly. Andrula promised immediately, and she even had a clear conscience. She never went down to the bay by herself. The old Katsika was always with her—for the first part of the way at least, as far as the shrubs went.

She took a piece of bread and some cheese and sat down in front of the gate, leaning her back against the wall so that she could see the water and the stars above, so like grapes in clusters and wreaths. Evangelia was doing her last chores in the yard. She had milked the goat and she brought a bowl of yoghurt and a plate of white beans for Andrula.

"Eat," she said. "You must be hungry."

"And, you?"

"I am not hungry."

She sat down next to her daughter and looked out at the sea. She seemed very tired and hardly spoke. She only sighed softly once or twice. But Andrula was used to her mother's sighing; she hardly heard it at all.

"Manula," she said when her plate was empty. "Do you know there is a third island between Ryos and Anti-Ryos? But it is much farther away and you can only see it when the sun goes down."

"Yes, I know," answered her mother.

"What kind of an island is it, Manula?"

"I don't know. But the people who have been there have nothing good to say about it."

"Who has been there?"

"The fishermen. Nobody from here goes to that island. It is desolate and barren, and there isn't even a house on it as far as I know, and no water. Once in a while a boat will stop there, but it never stays for long."

"Why not, Manula?"

"Oh, nobody feels comfortable there. Sotiris the fisherman has often talked about it. It was, he said, as if they were being watched, he and his people, as long as they were on the island. They had the feeling that somebody was staring at their backs the whole time. Sotiris is a brave man, and he searched the whole island, but there was nobody there, not a soul, not even an animal."

"Oh," murmured Andrula, very disappointed.

"And yet Sotiris insists even to this day that the island was not quite deserted. There *was* something there, even though it could not be seen. But whatever it was did not want any Christians there, he said. It drove them off."

"How could it drive the fishermen off if it couldn't be seen? Did they hear anything?"

"No, nothing, as far as I know. They only had a feeling, and it grew stronger and stronger. They had to go back to their boat and sail away as quickly as possible, otherwise—"

"Yes? Otherwise?" asked Andrula breathlessly.

"Sotiris couldn't say. And the other two who were with him couldn't either. They were really afraid and couldn't get to their boat fast enough. Sotiris said he would never again set foot on this island. He calls it 'the island that does not want us.'"

"The island that does not want us," repeated Andrula, half frightened, half irresistibly attracted.

"Yes. But come now and help me with the mats. It's late and I have to get up early tomorrow morning. Dimitrina has asked me over for the whole day. She wants me to help her dye yarn."

Andrula jumped up, her heart rejoicing wildly. She would be free and unhindered. Nobody would stop her from running down to the cove! And then to the island filled with secrets, the island that did not want people.

But it wants me, thought Andrula, and her heart beat faster. I am invited.

8

Not far from Evangelia's house, in the middle of a field but only a short distance from the road, stood a white chapel. This chapel, plain and modest as it was, was known throughout Kalonysos. It was dedicated to the Virgin Mary and everyone who needed help went there to ask it. For that reason the chapel was also called Our Lady of Mercy. Its real name was Panagia in the Fields, and Andrula's mother had a third name for it: Panagia Gitonissa—The Most Holy of Neighbors. Every week she went to the little church to clean the lamps in front of the old darkened wooden picture of the Virgin and fill them with fresh oil, and to sweep the small, almost empty room. Whenever she could afford to she lit a candle, a thin and inexpensive one for half a drachma. She seldom did this because even half a drachma was a lot of money for Evangelia. But every time she went she took at least one beautiful flower or some fragrant leaves from her flowerpots, and she had taught her little daughter to do the same.

The first day that Andrula had taken the goat out to

pasture she had quickly turned off the road and run into the church. She had placed a small twig from their rosemary bush and two small roses before the icon, crossed herself piously, and run off with an easy heart. But the next morning she was too eager to get to the cove where her new friend was waiting, and today, too, she passed the chapel even though her mother had called after her, "Take the Gitonissa a flower! I can't go to her today!"

Andrula had nodded, but she wasn't listening, and now she hurried past. Poor Katsika, too, was driven on even more mercilessly than the day before. Andrula knew that she would be too early at the cove but still she could not help herself. She just couldn't wait. The call of the sea and the secret island was too strong.

To make up for it she gave Katsika all her bread. She kept the cheese and the salty olives for herself. Uncertainly she looked from one to the other; without bread what was she to do with them? She could not take anything along with her. She would get awfully hungry, that was certain, because the grapes were of course for the dolphin. Finally she told herself that she could eat the cheese while he ate the grapes—she hoped he wouldn't want to play the grape game too long!—but the olives she would hide in a hole between two big rocks. They could stay there, they would keep. Poverty had taught her to be careful with even the smallest morsel of food.

Just when she had found a suitable crack she heard a swishing and splashing behind her. The dolphin had come. Happily she jumped down onto the smooth rock.

"Good morning!" she called out. "Good morning! Here are your grapes!"

"Take them with you," he said. "We have no time for games now. It is a long way to the island."

Take the grapes with her! Andrula looked at him in surprise. "How can I hold on, with just one hand?"

"How do you expect to hold on?" asked the dolphin, amused. "Do I have a mane like a horse? Or did you bring reins?"

Andrula did not even have a belt which could have served as a rein. She couldn't imagine how she was going to hold herself on the smooth back of the fish. But the dolphin only gurgled.

"Come," he said. "Leave your dress here. You won't need it. It would only get wet."

Andrula slipped out of her gray dress, rolled it up and hid it as well as she could. She stuffed as much of the cheese into her mouth as she could swallow in a hurry. The rest, just a little piece, she placed in the crack with the olives.

Now she was ready. She carefully climbed down the smooth rock as the dolphin directed her, the big bunch of grapes in her hand. The next step down was quite deep under water and from here it was easy to mount. The big fish kept very still, and there she sat, astride, right behind his head with its funny snout. She pressed his flanks with her knees because he said that was the way to sit tight.

At first she was frightened. Everything happened so fast! More than anything in the world she wanted something to hold on to—anything, a ribbon, or even one of the long pieces of seaweed that storms sometimes washed ashore. But she soon realized that she was in no danger. The dolphin swam smoothly with an even speed close to the surface.

With the growing security came the joy of the ride over the sea. How easy, how free this gliding was in the coolness and quiet, far more beautiful than riding in a boat. Andrula had done that just once in her life when Fotis, Sotiris' son, had taken a number of boys and girls for a ride in the bay. The oars had creaked and the heavy old boat had been slow, almost cumbersome, in making its way across the smooth water. Yet at that time Andrula had thought there was nothing more beautiful than such a ride. Now she was finding out that there was something far, far more beautiful. To ride across the sea on a dolphin was like being a boat itself, a small, fast boat with a high sail driven toward its destination by a fresh breeze. It was like gliding, it was like flying —yes, she was fish and bird at the same time. In her joy Andrula began to sing, just as they all had done that time in Fotis' old boat:

"A ship came from Chios . . ."

The dolphin gurgled deep in his throat and gave forth a soft, low whistle. Like all of his kind he loved happy, easy melodies almost as much as fish for breakfast, lunch and dinner. He often swam great distances to hear music, and sometimes he and his brothers would follow a ship for miles when a radio was playing on

deck. When Andrula had finished her song, he begged, "Go on singing! But something quiet, please. Because if I hear something lively, I can't help it—I have to leap, and that would be bad for you."

Ryos and Anti-Ryos were already behind them, a pale blue now. The sea shone and shimmered in the midday light, and for the first time Andrula really saw her island, rising as if newly created from the clear water. But it was smaller than she had imagined. Soon she could see that its craggy cliffs dropped sharply down to the sea. And how strange! It was almost— But it couldn't be! The island seemed to be moving toward them.

Possible or impossible, Andrula was happy about it. As gay as the dolphin ride had been at first, cool and silky as the sea was, now the sun stood higher, aiming its burning rays at Andrula's head and her unprotected shoulders. Why hadn't she worn a scarf? The glare of the water hurt her eyes.

"We are almost there," comforted the dolphin.

But at that moment something white and shiny shot through the blue water. A small face with large greenish eyes came up right beside them.

"The gorgona!" cried Andrula, frightened. Quickly, before the fabulous creature could do anything, she said what had to be said in this situation if one was to save one's life. "The great Alexander lives and rules!" she called out loudly and clearly.

"Who lives and rules?" asked the creature, very surprised.

"Your brother," said Andrula, who had taken her for
the mysterious sister of Alexander the Great.

"I have forty-nine sisters," said the nereid, gliding
effortlessly alongside the dolphin, "but as far as I know,
no brother. Who is this Alexander?"

The clear sea whirled and half a dozen of the forty-
nine sisters came to the surface, arm in arm and each
as beautiful as the next.

"Yes, tell us about this Alexander," they shouted cheerfully.

"Girls, girls," scolded the dolphin. "First let her go
on land! Can't you see how tired she is, how the sun
has worn her out?"

Sevenfold laughter sprang up. It seemed terribly funny
to these creatures of the sea that anybody could be tired
by the water or have to remain on the surface when
the sun got too strong.

"Go ahead, laugh!" said the dolphin. "You can laugh
here! But climb onto the land with her and see how
long you last!"

One of the seven nymphs came closer. "Give her
to us! We will carry her ashore in our arms."

"Oh no," said the dolphin firmly. "I found her. I'll
take her to Hyria, and back again, do you understand?"

They laughed once more. It sounded like the clinking
of glass. But they stopped asking for Andrula, and
swam playfully, chattering alongside them until they

reached the first brown and buff rocks. Many white arms lifted Andrula onto a stone in the shade of an over-hanging ledge.

"Welcome to Hyria! And now, tell us about our great brother of whom we know nothing."

9

At first Andrula was blinded, because she had come from the brightest light into deep shade. The blood pounded in her temples. She took a couple of deep breaths and felt better. The air was sweet and fresh on this island of Hyria, as the dolphin and these peculiar girls had called it.

The island that did not want people? Andrula did not feel at all like that, nor were there any invisible, hostile eyes watching her. On the contrary, she felt very much at home here. The stone on which she sat supported her just as willingly as the smooth rock at home in the little cove.

"The great Alexander," she began. "Yes, he was a king and a hero a long time ago, even before the Turks made slaves of us Greeks. He went with his soldiers across the sea and conquered many lands. Wherever he went he brought everything under his power—towns, villages, all of Asia Minor. But I don't know the names of all those distant places."

"It doesn't matter," said one of the nereids. They

had arranged themselves in a half circle in front of her, making an arc of bright, attentive faces above pretty, slender arms. They relaxed as comfortably in the water as people do on a green lawn.

"He had a sister," Andrula went on, "who loved him more than anything in the world. But during a storm she fell off his ship into the sea, and he lost her. That is what the fishermen tell at home. She did not drown but turned into a mermaid, a gorgona. She has the body of a fish. In one hand she holds a trident and in the other hand a sailboat. Calliope, the wife of the coffeehouse owner, has a picture of her, embroidered in colored silks, hanging on the wall, under glass. I have seen it many times."

"But this Alexander, what happened to him?" asked all the seven nereids together.

"He died. I think he was still quite young," answered Andrula sadly.

"But you said that he lives and rules!" cried the chorus of crystal voices.

"Yes, that's what you have to say. The gorgona is still swimming in the sea and hoping to find her brother. Sometimes she comes to the surface and calls out to a ship: 'Is the great Alexander alive?' And then one has to answer immediately: 'The great Alexander lives and rules!' Because if you tell the truth—that he is long since dead and buried—then she gets terribly angry and makes huge waves and pulls the ship to the bottom."

"Oh, nonsense," said the nymphs to each other. "We, and our cousins the winds, are the ones who do that.

Do you know what, sisters? This gorgona does not even exist."

"And if she did exist," one of them said, jumping up in the water, "how stupid she must be to believe such lies over and over again!"

With that they lost all interest in the gorgona and turned once more to the dolphin. "Give us this little human being, dolphin, and let us play with it."

"Oh no," said Andrula's friend firmly. "This little human being is going to have a look around the island now." While Andrula was talking he had been swimming back and forth slowly with quick and watchful eyes.

Andrula remembered that she was still holding the grapes in her hand.

"No, first this!" she cried. "Catch!" And she threw the first one. The water nymphs returned. "Us too, us too!" they shouted.

"Shall I give them some?" Andrula asked the dolphin.

"I don't care," he gurgled. "But they don't like grapes, they just want to play with them. You will see."

Andrula threw her grapes near and far, and there was a cheerful fight as to who would catch them. The first grapes disappeared into the mouths of the nereids, who spat them out in disgust.

"They are sweet!" It was obvious that they preferred salty things. After this they were contented to try to catch the grapes before the dolphin caught them and to let him leap many times for them. But he was as quick and agile as they were.

Andrula laughed as she watched all this, but she was sorry to see all the grapes go. They were so cool, so sweet and fresh, and she was thirsty. She plucked one for herself, and then another. "I am terribly thirsty," she apologized to the dolphin.

"Thirsty?" cried one of the nymphs. "With all this water here?"

"Yes, salt water!" said Andrula contemptuously.

"But that is the best thing about it." The nereid laughed. She did a somersault, disappeared and came up again between two of her sisters.

"If you are thirsty," said the dolphin, "you should go to the spring and drink."

"To the spring?" asked Andrula in surprise. "But the island is barren and dry, the fisherman Sotiris said!"

"The fisherman Sotiris can't have seen much of the island. How would he know? Go on, follow the path up there around the rock. It will lead you to the water."

"Is it safe?" asked Andrula, a little afraid to venture alone to the interior of the island.

"Aren't you the guest of Hyria?" answered the dolphin. "The guest is sacred. Go along, but come back soon. I will be waiting for you."

Reassured, she nodded and climbed quickly from stone to stone. When she reached the top of the cliff she turned around and waved to the dolphin. The water was so clear that she could see his large shape as through glass. The nereids had swum away. Only two of them could still be seen, their hair lying on the dark blue water like light brown seaweed.

The path was only a small trail winding along the steep coastline, soon to turn farther inland. Andrula was surprised to see how green the hills were. There was hardly any grass, but the ground was covered with curly short herbs which gave off a strong scent as soon as her feet touched them. She recognized thyme, marjoram, and even a certain low-growing form of mint, and in between were all the little red, blue, and violet flowers which had finished blooming at home about the end of April.

Whatever had Sotiris meant when he called this place hostile? It was the happiest, gayest place in the whole world. You had only to breathe and its golden cheerfulness ran through all your veins. Andrula laughed out loud at the fisherman, because he was stupid and had thoroughly misunderstood the island of Hyria.

There was the spring right in front of her. Thirsty as she was, she had to stop for a moment and marvel. She had never seen such a beautiful place in all her life.

Hyria's spring poured forth from among great white stones and ran into a basin, the bottom of which was covered with colored pebbles. Each of these brown, purple, yellow, and bluish pebbles shimmered like jewels under the clear ripples. They looked like fruit, like figs, mulberries, and grapes.

How cold the water was! And sweet. Never in her life had Andrula tasted such water. She scooped it up with both hands and cooled her face. Then she sat down on the grass, her hands around her knees, and followed with her eyes the silver trickle as it splashed down and wandered through a little vale.

Her eyes opened wide. Down there, where the water wound its way into a second, somewhat larger basin, wasn't that like the hem of a many-pleated white gown? A slender, graceful, almost transparent figure rose, shimmered, smiled, and disappeared.

Andrula knew for certain that she had not fallen asleep and seen this figure in her dreams. She had heard the nightingale singing all along, over there in the oleander bush! Or could one hear a real nightingale in one's dreams?

That was something else to think about. A nightingale, in September? But anything seemed to be possible on this island.

She stood up and went to the spot where she thought she had seen the figure. She stopped respectfully a couple of steps away and said softly but very clearly: "My lady, I thank you for the water! It is the best water in the world."

Then she went back to the fountain, broke off two pale red anemones and tossed them into the basin. The spring murmured and chattered through its stones, playing with the flowers until they spun around in the center of the pool.

So she felt she had done the right thing. Contented and with a light heart, the girl ran back to her friend.

"Callisto herself," said the dolphin, impressed, when she told him what she had seen. "The Nymph of the

Spring. She rarely appears. She must have wanted to welcome you."

Andrula nodded. She realized that a great honor had been bestowed upon her.

The ride home across the sea seemed short to her. This was fortunate, because again the sun was burning with all its might, and Andrula was glad when she was standing on her rock once more.

"Are you coming again with me tomorrow?" asked the dolphin as she thanked him.

"Tomorrow." She remembered that the next day was Sunday. "No, I don't think Mother will let me go out. But the day after tomorrow, early, will you wait here for me? Please!"

He dived two, three times in quick succession, as if he were nodding.

"Oh, my dolphin, the time will seem so long!" said Andrula. And he nodded once more in his special way as if to say: "To me too."

10

Nereids, the Nymph of the Spring, her dolphin . . . Andrula had enough, more than enough, to keep her mind occupied for the whole Sunday. Over and over she lived through every moment of her trip. She saw every scene again, heard every word, smelled and tasted the fragrance and the water of the island and the salt of the waves. All day she felt an urgent impatience to go back again. Never had a Sunday seemed so long.

It was always the quietest day in the little house behind the dunes. The loom did not clatter. No work was done except washing up the dishes. In the afternoon a neighbor might come and lean on the wall and say a couple of words, or Evangelia would walk with her daughter across the fields to one of the other houses after the greatest heat had passed. In the evening Andrula was permitted to go into the village for an hour and play. That was the way it had always been, but it was so no longer.

She went to church with her mother as usual, neat and clean in her Sunday dress. Evangelia had woven it herself with a design of white threads above the hem and on the little pockets. As they arrived at the church Stassa appeared with her mother. Stassa wore a new dress of shiny rayon, white with thick red rosebuds. She frowned when she saw her enemy, raised her head arrogantly and looked right past her.

Andrula smiled. Let Stassa have a new dress, and what if it was covered with a thousand red roses! What was that compared to her own adventures? She threw back her head, even prouder than Stassa. After all, she had traveled. Stassa had never even been away from Kalonysos.

After church Evangelia walked over to her sister-in-law.

"How are you, Stamatina," she said in a friendly voice. "These two have had a fight. Come on, girls, shake hands."

Andrula hesitated, but her mother pushed her forward.

At that moment Stassa remarked so loudly that everybody could hear her: "I don't have to shake hands with a beggar brat."

"What are you saying?" cried Andrula's aunt, shocked and embarrassed. But Evangelia only said, "Come Andrula," and walked with her daughter down the main street to her house without a word. They had to stop at the baker's to pick up their Sunday dinner which had been cooking in the baker's oven. As soon as they passed the last houses Evangelia's steps quickened as if she could not wait to get home. Andrula had trouble keeping up with her. And then her mother closed the little gate as if to shut out the whole world—the gate which always stood open during the daytime.

"Lay the table, Andrula," she said sharply. She went into the room to change her clothes, because her only good dress had to be preserved, even on a Sunday.

When her mother reappeared Andrula noticed that she had been crying. Her face looked drawn and she hardly spoke. She ate little of the stuffed tomatoes and she did not lie down after dinner as she usually did, but went to her loom.

"Mama!" cried Andrula, horrified. "On Sunday?"

"If people can wag their lying tongues on Sunday, then I can do honest work," said Evangelia. It sounded as if anger were choking her voice. "Let me be, child," she added more mildly. "I have to do *something*. But you lie down."

Andrula was so ashamed that her face burned. The clanking of the loom seemed twice as loud in the Sunday quiet. Everyone in the Chora would surely hear it! How could her mother do such a thing? Now surely everybody would be saying that they were so pitifully poor that they even had to work on the Sabbath. Should she run down to the shore so that the neighbors would see it was her mother who was not honoring Sunday, that she herself had nothing to do with it?

But then she steeled her heart. Why should she care what people said about her and her mother! And she would not waste even the smallest word on Stassa, never again in her life.

"Go to sleep, Andrula," said her mother once more.

Andrula fetched the mat and spread it on the floor and lay down. Broodingly her eyes followed the shuttle as it shot through the white chain with its red thread. After a while her mother asked, "Are you asleep, little one?" Her voice was no longer angry, but rather sad and thoughtful.

"No, Manula," answered the girl, and she propped herself up.

"You know," continued her mother, "you must not hold it against Stassa. She only repeats what she has heard. And the whole village knows that Aunt Stamatina talks first and thinks later.

"Then I hold it against Aunt Stamatina," declared Andrula stubbornly.

"She never did like me," said Evangelia sadly. "Oh, Andrula, what kind of life is this we lead? What is to become of us, you and me?"

Andrula was astonished. Become? What else should become of them but what they were now, mother and daughter? And what kind of life was it? It was a wonderful life. Maybe a little bitter today, but tomorrow . . .

Tomorrow she would go to the island, tomorrow, tomorrow! Soon Andrula was asleep.

Evangelia went on weaving and thought of nothing but her worries. Now not only she herself was bitterly lonely but her child too. Almost all the people of the Chora were poor. The whole island was poor. Yet as soon as one of them had a little more than the others he fancied himself far, far better. Just because they had so little, nothing meant so much to them as money and possessions.

Andrula was still young. But in three or four years, what then? The bedspread she was weaving right now was ordered for the dowry of a fourteen-year-old girl. Every mother in the village began to collect bed and table linen as soon as a daughter was born. For one had to marry off a daughter, and try to marry her off as well as possible. That meant a good dowry, and a piece of land, and some livestock.

Andrula had nothing, nothing at all, neither linen nor carpets, nor land, nor livestock. Who would marry a girl like that, poor as she was? No one.

Evangelia knew no other way but to prepare her little daughter as soon as possible for a hard and lonely life. She had to learn to care for herself. Tomorrow she would show her how to weave.

11

That same evening, when Evangelia told Andrula her decision, she met with passionate resistance. Andrula fought her with all her might. No, no, no, she did not want to learn how to weave! She did not want to and she wouldn't.

Evangelia had expected some rebellion, because she knew how little her daughter liked to sit still. But that she would refuse so violently, Evangelia had not foreseen.

"You have to learn sometime," she said helplessly. "What else are you going to do when you grow up? How are you going to earn your living?"

"When I grow up I'll go to sea like my father," declared Andrula.

"Girls don't go to sea," answered her mother curtly.

"Girls like me do go to sea!" Andrula stamped her foot as if to ram her decision into the ground, and added even more stubbornly, "Anyhow, it's vacation time now."

"The vacations are much too long." Her mother

sighed. She stopped weaving and picked up her scarf. "Come, let's go to the chapel. I was too tired yesterday to fill the lamps. Please carry the oil. Where are the matches?"

Andrula found the matches. Slowly they went down the dusty path along the fields. Her mother carried a small bouquet of geranium leaves with a tiny, almost completely round dark red dahlia in the center. She placed her modest offering before the picture of the Virgin and stood in front of it for a while. The Most Holy One looked down at her with her large, dark eyes.

Andrula busied herself with the lamps. She was ill at ease. She felt almost embarrassed in front of the ancient picture. She had nothing to say to it, and she wished her mother wouldn't pray quite so long. She wished that it would get dark very soon, that she could go to sleep, and that the new day would come quickly. But that was nothing to pray for. Yet when she looked at the picture she felt as if the Gitonissa knew exactly what was in her mind.

Back home, the teacher's wife was waiting at the door for them. Her laundry woman, Asimina, had fallen ill, and she needed Evangelia's help tomorrow and the next day.

Naturally Evangelia agreed; she wanted to do it— anything. Even the smallest earning was welcome. Andrula rejoiced. Nothing would come of the weaving lesson tomorrow after all—and of course not on Tuesday

either. Nobody began anything new on a Tuesday. Tuesday was a bad day for beginnings.

"You stay home," Mother decided, "and wash my colored things. I can take the larger pieces with me."

She left early Monday morning, carrying her own bundle of laundry on her head. Andrula hardly took the time to wave after her. She pulled bucket after bucket of water out of the well as fast as she could to fill the large copper kettle which stood in the corner on two or three flat stones. Then she lit the twigs underneath.

Andrula ran for more wood while the water heated slowly, took the goat out and put her on a rope underneath the bushes. She fetched the shallow wooden tub and ran for the soap. It was green soap, coarse and hard, the only kind Andrula knew. And then she rubbed and rubbed on the wooden washboard. She splashed and splashed until all the spots were out. Now the rinsing!

Soon the wash hung in the bright sunshine and Andrula hurried off, taking the shortest way to the little cove. Climbing across the rocks, she spotted her friend far out in the water. He had just come up for air and he saw her at once.

He whistled at her. "Stay there! You can easily mount from those rocks!"

"No, no," Andrula shouted back. "Suppose someone should see me!"

She did not stop until she had rounded the sharp rock which protected her from curious eyes. Only then

did she slip off her dress. She hid it well and climbed
onto the dolphin's back. She kept her scarf on her head
today. It was a large thin one which also protected her
shoulders.

This second ride was very easy. Nothing could be
more delightful than to glide like this through the waves.
Yes, thought Andrula, when I grow up I'll go to sea.
She told the dolphin and the news made him so happy
that he would have loved to leap high over the next
wave. But he controlled himself in time. His little friend
would never want to ride with him across the sea again
if he played such a trick on her.

A similar thought had crossed Andrula's mind. "My
dolphin," she asked, "what would happen to me if I
fell off your back?"

"Then I would save you," he answered immediately.
"We used to do that quite often. Of course we did it
only for special people who had fallen or been pushed
into the water. We used to help good people who had
been thrown overboard by bad people. Like Arion."

"Who was he?" asked Andrula curiously, hoping to
hear one of his beautiful stories.

"I'll tell you another time," said the dolphin. "It's not comfortable to talk during a ride."

Andrula was content. They were already approaching the island. She began to look for the nereids, but there were none to be seen.

The dolphin swam slowly now as they came to a sandy spot between two tall rocks. It was not much bigger than a sea shell, but here the water was shallow; Andrula could easily climb down and wade to the island. Not a living thing could be seen except some sea gulls.

Andrula sat down on the fine white sand and unfastened a little bag which she had carried around her neck. She loosened the string and the largest and most beautiful of her grapes appeared.

"Oh," said the dolphin, surprised and delighted. "So you did not forget them!"

"Did you think I would?" answered Andrula reproachfully. She threw the first fat, green-golden grape. "There, that's my ticket."

"What is a ticket?" inquired the dolphin.

"One needs a ticket to go on a big ship to Athens,"

explained Andrula, proud to be able to teach him something.

"And if you don't have one?" he asked.

"Then the ship will not take you along," said Andrula. "Without a ticket the sailor wouldn't even let you go aboard!"

"Which sailor?" asked the dolphin.

"The one who stands at the gangplank and asks for the tickets," Andrula told him patiently. She plucked one grape after another and threw them to him. It was much quieter without the nereids and they could have a sensible talk.

The dolphin understood now. "Aha," he said, very pleased with himself. "This ticket is the pay the captain demands for taking you across the sea."

"Right," said Andrula.

"And is the ticket gold or silver?"

"Oh no, it is only a piece of paper," explained Andrula. "But one has to pay money for it."

"And what is that—money?"

"You don't know that? If you have it, then you are rich and wear shiny clothes from the store and a real golden ring with a pink stone. If you don't have it, then you are poor, like my mother and me."

"Now I understand," said the dolphin. "The world really hasn't changed much even though a couple of thousand years have passed since the god came across the sea. But Andrula," he went on, "you know that there is no need for the grapes, that I'm your captain because we are friends?"

"Oh yes, my dolphin," said Andrula. "I know that as well as you do. I bring the grapes because you like them."

"Then everything is all right," said the dolphin contentedly. "Go on now and explore the island. I'll swim around and fish a bit. I haven't had my breakfast yet."

Far out at sea there was a brown sail and he urged the girl not to walk along the high cliff so she wouldn't be seen. "Go straight inland," he advised her. "It is a little longer that way but that doesn't matter. You can't get lost because all paths on Hyria lead to Callisto's Spring."

Andrula nodded, and he swam off.

12

This time Andrula did not go to the spring empty-handed. She picked some flowers on the way and wove them loosely into a wreath which she put into the lower basin, bowing politely before she drank the water.

But as she bent down, she stopped short. In front of her, in the damp ground, she could see several clear and sharp hoof prints.

Andrula sat back on her heels and studied them. They were hoof prints all right, smaller than Katsika's but just as sharply chiseled. They must be from a young goat or a lamb.

What had the fisherman Sotiris said? There were neither man nor beast on this deserted island? Well, he had been wrong before when he said the island was arid and that it did not welcome anybody on its soil. Really, that Sotiris! Oh well, fishermen and their yarns, you just could not believe them. She would look for herself now and find out, if she could, the story behind the hoof tracks.

She drank of the sweet, sparkling spring water and

then climbed up the slope to where the spring gushed out. Slowly she circled the hill. The grass was soft under her feet and she was careful not to loosen any stones.

This caution was justified, for soon she heard, quite close, what sounded like the happy sound of school boys wrestling. She was not far from the top now. Some large rocks were right in front of her. They would keep her hidden. Silently she crept on. She ducked and lay down flat, then looked carefully out of her hiding place.

Below her was a small valley, from which came the noises she had heard. Four boys were playing down there, two against two, in a lively contest. One of them rode on the shoulders of another and tried to pull his opponent down.

Andrula knew that game. The big boys played it at home, but mostly in the water. That way they did not fall so hard. But these four here on Hyria . . .

Andrula's eyes suddenly grew very big. She had never seen boys like this! Now she knew what had made those tracks near the spring. Those were live, tanned boys down there, from their curly hair down to their hips, but from the hips down they had shaggy fur and slender goats' legs.

She forgot to breathe as she stared with all her might at the odd creatures. She breathed again only when the game ended with both riders falling down amid great hilarity. Quickly she slipped away and arrived at the cliffs completely out of breath. She forgot the brown sail and started to wave to the dolphin as soon as she reached the edge. He came close at once and asked with concern if something had happened to her.

"Boys," panted Andrula, fanning herself with her kerchief. "Four boys with goats' legs!"

"And that is why you ran so fast?" gurgled the dolphin. "Were you afraid of them? They are not even as big as you are."

"I wasn't really afraid," answered Andrula, still out of breath. "Not afraid, but . . . but . . ."

"The goats' legs," he said understandingly. "A little unusual, I must admit. But I had thought the unusual, here on Hyria, wouldn't be anything new to you. A spring which changes into a nymph . . . half a dozen nereids . . ."

"The nereids look like me," objected Andrula.

"That is only on the surface," said the dolphin. "You would be surprised if you knew them better. That reminds me. Don't let them talk you into anything, do you understand? Don't ever let them tempt you into visiting their grottoes at the bottom of the sea! They know very well that human beings who go down there must drown. They don't care, or else they always forget. But you can trust the little fauns in the valley as you can trust any other creatures you might meet on the island."

"All right, if you say so," said Andrula obediently. "But now I would rather go home and leave the trusting until tomorrow."

But even that was easier said than done. Andrula must have spent half an hour the next day hiding behind her rock, and still she could not find the courage to climb down to the four fauns.

This half hour had been anything but boring. The little goat-legged creatures down there were so deeply involved in their games it was wonderful to watch them. When they did not bump into each other they turned somersaults or played catch. Again and again they fell on top of one another, a mass of wriggling, kicking arms and legs. Andrula had to stuff her kerchief into her mouth to keep from laughing out loud.

Suddenly they seemed to have a new idea. One of them squatted on the ground and the others placed themselves in front of him. Andrula was curious, and she dared to push her head a little farther out.

She saw to her amazement that three of the boys put their arms around each other's shoulders, just as people do when they are beginning to dance. Now the fourth one clapped his hands in rhythm and they began to sing. Well! thought Andrula, everything is just like it is at home in the Chora!

She watched with interest, and very critically. She completely forgot that she wanted to remain hidden. Even though the song was strange and the words did not carry up to her, she could see what dance they were doing. It was a Syrtos, or was supposed to be one. But at school they could do it better! Much better, thought Andrula, who felt qualified to judge. Wasn't she the best dancer in her class? Didn't she always have to lead when their teacher gave them a dancing lesson instead of gymnastics? That was one thing in which she was really ahead of Stassa. Stassa could sing higher and shriller than any other girl, but when it came to dancing she lacked something. It was the rhythm, the beat, the ease. Andrula, on the other hand, was light on her feet, and she danced rather like a boy, always inventing new steps.

So she was completely absorbed when the four fauns began another dance. But what was that supposed to be? Such awful hopping! Andrula shook her dark hair, getting angrier and angrier. Finally she could not stand it any longer. She jumped up.

"Hey!" she shouted. "You are doing it all wrong, you little goats down there!"

And with that she ran down the gentle slope.

13

The four dancers stood for a moment as if rooted. Then they crowded close together and looked at her—apparently not afraid, but very curious. This brought Andrula sharply to her senses and made her move closer, carefully, slower and slower. Finally she arrived at the edge of the dance floor and stood still, suddenly shy again.

The little group opposite her began to move as one toward her. They stopped right in front of her.

"We aren't goats," said the largest of the four boys. "And if you can dance any better than we can, why don't you show us? Who are you anyhow?"

"I am Andrula. The dolphin brought me here. He knows you, I think."

"Oh, the dolphin. Yes, then be welcome. My name is Melas. My brother here is Balios and this little one is Battos, because he stammers a bit. And this one here, who can hardly control his laughing, is Gelanor."

"Then I guess they call you Melas because of your black fur," remarked Andrula politely.

"That's right," said Melas, stroking his black shining flanks proudly. For a few minutes they just stood and looked at each other.

Three of the brown faces were narrow. Only little Battos' face was still full and round. Their eyes all looked much the same, very large, slightly slanting, and the color of clear, dark honey. Andrula saw, to her surprise, that tiny horns grew through their curly hair. But except for their goats' legs, they looked exactly like other boys their age, sinewy and strong, brown as hazelnuts, and full of mischief.

And the fauns saw in front of them a girl who could have been their sister—just as brown and thin, with hair as black as Melas', except that it was not curly, with a finely chiseled nose and a firm chin. The eyes, of course, were different—very dark, a beautiful, pure brown.

Now, as Andrula smiled, the four faces in front of her broke into smiles too, and the boys began to push each other forward. The smallest one, Battos, looked up at Andrula and the dimples near the corners of his mouth were so deep that she could have put her fingertips into them. He seemed to like the newcomer, who had such peculiar thin, smooth fur, from her shoulders down almost to her knees, a thin, smooth, pink fur! On her arms and legs this creature had sensible, firm, brown skin just like his. Funny.

Slowly they shoved and pushed until little Battos was close enough to reach out and touch this funny skin. He took a deep breath and grabbed Andrula's slip, which she had kept on instead of her dress because it was made of thin cotton and dried fast. He held a fold carefully between thumb and forefinger and looked questioningly at the girl.

"Battos wants to know what kind of skin that is," explained Melas, who wanted to know too.

"But this is not skin," said Andrula. "This is my petticoat."

"Does it grow on you like our fur grows on us?" asked Balios.

"Of course not," answered Andrula, laughing.

Gelanor was immediately infected by the laughter. "Of course not!" he repeated two or three times as if it were the funniest thing in the world.

Andrula thought they had had enough of staring, and started to talk about the dancing, for that was her main interest.

"Well," she began, "this Tsamikos that you were dancing before—"

"This what?" asked Melas, Balios and Gelanor all at the same time, while Battos grew a deep red from strain but could not get out a sound, not in time, that is.

"The Tsamikos," repeated Andrula. "The second dance. You were just doing it when I came down."

"That is its name?" marveled Melas.

"Yes, that is what we call it," explained Andrula, astonished. "What do you call it?"

"Nothing," answered Melas, and this again sounded very funny to Gelanor.

"You don't know the name and you don't know how to do it," said Andrula dryly.

"How did you say it—Samtikos?" asked Balios carefully.

"Yes, almost." Andrula nodded seriously. "If you would put your hoofs—excuse me, feet I meant to say—no, but they are hoofs! Well . . ."

"Why don't you say hoofs," said Balios helpfully. His eyes twinkled as he added, "You can say 'graceful hoofs' or 'pretty hoofs' when just 'hoofs' doesn't seem polite to you."

Battos wanted to say something too, but it took awhile for him to get it out. Andrula looked at him expectantly, and that made it take even longer.

"F-f-fine," he finally blurted it out and pointed his finger at Andrula.

"How do you mean, fine?" objected Balios. "We haven't seen her do it yet."

But Battos had now gathered his courage, and there was no stopping him. "N-n-n-no." He shook his curly head. "F-fine talk. F-f-feet!"

"Aha," said Melas. "I know what he wants to say. He means it is easy for Andrula to talk, because she has feet, and they are better for dancing than hoofs."

Battos nodded, happy that he had been understood. The other three nodded too, because Battos had expressed their own opinions. But Andrula would not hear of it.

"Nonsense," she cried. "Hoofs or feet, that's neither here nor there. It is the rhythm, and knowing the right steps. For that you have to have a leader. Wait, I'll show you." And with that she ran up the hill where she had left her kerchief. She came right back and gave Melas one corner of it.

"Another one of those skins," he said, perplexed. "What am I supposed to do with it?"

"This is a scarf and not a skin," corrected Andrula. "Take it, and you others stand aside."

"Why the scarf?" insisted Melas.

"Because I can turn better with it," explained Andrula, and so he held the other corner. She twirled quickly under his raised arm, went down low, jumped up quickly, and turned gracefully again. "Do you see?" she asked.

Melas saw what she meant and nodded with the others.

"So," said Andrula, "let's begin with a Syrtos. That is the easiest dance." She began to sing her favorite song, the song about the ship from Chios which sailed to Samos, its two dinghies behind it. "Now let's start: one, two, three."

And away they danced in a half circle over the green grass.

At the second stanza the others began to hum too, and at the third one they knew the melody and sang heartily, even if it was only tra-la-la, tra-la-la, and after the fourth one they all cried, "Once again!" Even Battos with the heavy tongue—only he did not say it, he just sang it, for that he was able to do just as fast as his brothers.

Andrula taught them the words of the song, and then it went twice as well. "Really, that was much better," she praised them, and her pupils beamed. "But Battos," she continued, "you, as the last one, should put your free hand nicely on your back whenever you are not going click-click with your fingers."

Battos put his little brown hand on his back and looked at her expectantly. But no sooner had he done it than he had to take it away again to give it to Andrula as she took the last place. Now it was Melas' turn to be the leader.

Gelanor pushed himself forward. "No, Melas, let me!" His brother did not mind, and he gave him his place and the corner of the scarf. They started the song once again, and Gelanor started to jump like the little goat he was, at least half of him.

"Hey, hey, hey!" shouted four resentful voices. "What are you doing, Gelanor?"

He paid no attention, but whirled around, tried to throw both feet forward at the same time, and landed flat on the grass. Melas was pulled down with him, and Balios and Battos had trouble keeping themselves upright. Andrula folded her arms across her chest and shook her head reproachfully.

"There, you see—our hoofs," said Gelanor, jumping up.

"All I see is somebody who wants to run before he has learned to walk," remarked Andrula sternly.

"No, no," Gelanor assured her. "It is because of the

hoofs! You don't know how hard it is to dance if you have only two legs."

"I too have only two legs. I know exactly how it is," contradicted Andrula.

"Yes, but you have real feet down there, with toes on them," said Balios. And Battos nodded and beamed, because he had said it first.

"You must believe us," urged Melas in his quiet way. "It is really not so simple to be two different things—"

"Yes, you usually end up on the ground, and with a bang, too!" interrupted Balios, laughing.

"—one half a goat who has to jump, and one half a boy who wants to dance and sing," continued Melas. "Sometimes you get quite mixed up."

Andrula could see their point. "Well, now I am here and I can help you," she said. "We'll try it once more. Melas, you lead."

Melas took the scarf. This time Battos could put his hand obediently on his back because Andrula was not dancing. She stood before the boys, singing the song and clapping the beat with her hands. Melas did very well.

"Bravo, bravo!" Andrula praised him, and he bowed, his hand across his chest. Just at that moment Gelanor kicked his feet out from under him and the first real Syrtos ended in a lively scramble.

Just like the boys in the Chora—and now Andrula remembered that it was probably high time for her to be going home. She clapped her hands and the four scrambled up.

"Listen," she said when they quieted down. "I have to go home now."

"Home? Where is that. they asked, dismayed. "Aren't you going to stay with us always?"

"No," said Andrula. "I have to go back again to my own island." And as she said it a great sadness came over her that it had to be so, that she had to leave this happy island each time and go back to the arid fields, the drying wells, the naked poverty of Kalonysos, and to a life that was always commonplace.

But she realized right away that no one could be sad here on Hyria. "I'll be back," she promised, laughing "Good-bye," and she ran off, waving her scarf.

The four fauns galloped after her, shouting and waving. "Stay with us, Andrula! Come back tomorrow! Don't forget!"

They were still standing high on the cliff and waving as Andrula glided through the waves on the dolphin. "Have a good trip," they cried, "have a good trip!"

14

Andrula found herself once more holding the position that Stassa had taken away from her, and she accepted it as her natural, indisputable right. She greatly enjoyed leading the fauns, and they enjoyed it just as much. They were ready for any game Andrula suggested, and it never occurred to them to argue or to say, "No, we don't want to play this today, but something else." They were far too curious for that. But when Andrula began to teach them more difficult dances she found that even on Hyria you had to have patience.

They skipped, they jumped—heart and soul was in their dancing. And yet they would mistake right for left, front for back, and finally fell again and again over their own clumsy feet, especially Gelanor.

"Do you know something?" she often sighed. "You don't just have two legs, you have two left legs!"

That sounded so funny to them that it finished the lesson for the day. Everything turned into complete joyous chaos. And so Andrula had to think of something else. She insisted that her goat-legged pupils learn to sing their dancing songs first, verse for verse, word for word. She was successful, for even Battos, whose tongue was so slow, sang in a pure and clear voice. And because the life depicted by these songs was so utterly alien to them Andrula kept having to explain. The singing hour turned into a story hour almost every time.

"Today we are going to learn a new dance," she would begin. "It is called the Gerakina."

"What is a Gerakina?" one of the brothers would want to know immediately, usually Melas or Balios.

"A girl like I am, only older," Andrula would explain. "She went to the well for water and she fell in."

Now they did not know what a well was because on Hyria there was only Callisto's Spring, and anyone who fell into it would only scrape his nose on the other side —nothing else. So now she had to describe a well. This done, Andrula could sing the song for them. It was a lovely song and the four of them listened with shining eyes and ears pricked up.

> "Gerakina at the well
> Gerakina runs to fill her water jug
> Run, Gerakina, run!
> How her bangles ring—
> Drun drun, drun drun drun—"

The boys liked that. "Drun drun, drun drun drun," they hummed happily all through the second stanza, which told of Gerakina's fall into the well and her loud cry for help. The boys understood this without any further explanation, but they did not react the way Andrula would have expected. They thought it was funny and doubled up in laughter at this unfortunate accident.

"It is nothing to laugh at!" scolded Andrula. "I would like to see you fall into a well and still feel like laughing!"

"All four of us?" asked Balios.

"One would be enough," said Andrula. "But I know you! One of you would be sitting down in the cold, wet well and the others would be doing somersaults for joy up here."

"There are no wells on the island," said Balios. He almost sounded sorry about it.

"Fortunately," said Andrula dryly. "Otherwise you might try it."

The four rascals in front of her grinned broadly, but they didn't say anything.

"Well, let's go on: The young man who sings this song runs to the well—the whole village runs to the well—and he calls from afar:

"Gerakina,
I will pull you out!
And I'll make you my wife—"

"Why?" Balios wanted to know.

"Why? Because he loves her, of course," explained Andrula, growing impatient.

"Loves her—what is that?"

"That is . . . that is . . . oh, you wouldn't understand. It doesn't really matter. Anyhow, he lets a golden rope down, catches her at the belt and pulls her up—"

"And her bracelets jingle!" chimed the boys triumphantly.

"Exactly. And now let's try the dance. Twelve steps this time: six forward—one, two, three, four, five, six—and six back again. It's quite simple. Gelanor, the right foot crosses over the left foot—over! Gelanor, how often have I told you, when I say 'over' I don't mean 'behind'!"

But he would probably never learn.

Once in a while Andrula felt more like staying with her dolphin rather than teaching clumsy little fauns to dance.

"Run off, my little goats, run and play! Not today," was all she had to say when the boys came racing toward her. They did not mind in the least. Everyone could do as he pleased here on Hyria.

Andrula would sit on the sun-warmed rock and listen to the dolphin's stories. The big fish would swim slowly back and forth, as near to her as possible, and tell her of the wonderful gardens deep at the bottom of the sea, of colorful springs and strange fish and swarms of sea horses. "Andrula, Andrulitsa," he would say, "if only you could come down with me and see for yourself!"

Sometimes as he was talking the sunlight seemed to gather into white flowers far out at sea, come closer, and change into the faces of the nereids—one, two, or many of them—and it would grow noisy and lively around Andrula and the dolphin. Their crystal laughter would fill the air.

When that happened the fauns ran away without being told, because they would have nothing to do with these sea creatures. They found them boring and their silvery voices, they said, made them feel cold.

Andrula, though, could sit for hours on her rock and watch the nereids' games. How graceful they were! And not only their voices--everything about them was silvery. Every pleat of their short, light gowns was like a silver veil.

Again and again they tried to coax Andrula down into the water with them. But the large fish watched over her. They laughed and chided him and called him a dreary old spoilsport.

"The little one will burn to a crisp in that sun," they scolded, as if they were only concerned with An-drula's welfare.

But the dolphin turned with a quick flip of his tail and drove them apart by pushing his mighty head right into the middle of them. They swam off, jeering, but Andrula was always amazed to see them return all smiles and sweet words. Didn't a "No" mean anything to them?

Was it because of the stories her friend told, or because of the untiring efforts of the nereids? Andrula was more and more tempted to get down into the water and dance and play like them, or at least to swim safely here in this little cove.

"Dolphin," she said one day when they were alone, and she followed it up with a deep sigh.

He came closer immediately. "What is the matter, Andrula? Is anything wrong?"

"Oh, no. Only—if I could swim like you!"

"Like me?" he gurgled, amused. "You are mighty ambitious. But to swim like a human being—that you could easily learn."

"Do you really think so?"

"Certainly, and better than most," he said without hesitation. "We have only to watch that none of the nereids are nearby when we try it. And Andrula, you have to promise me once more that you will never dive down into their grotto with them, even after you know how to swim."

"Definitely not, I promise you. My father was lost at sea. I know that it is dangerous for us."

"So? Your father was lost at sea? Was he a sailor?"

"He was a sponge diver. He went out with one of the boats and never came back. That was a long time ago. I never knew him."

"Does it make you sad to talk about it?"

"Not here. Nobody can be sad on this island. But my mother is often sad."

For a moment the sorrow of her mother touched her heart like a finger gently knocking. But she did not want to listen.

"Shall we start right away?" Andrula jumped up, her eyes sparkling with excitement.

"Wait a minute," warned the dolphin. He swam a

few wide circles and came back, reassured. "Not a trace of them," he reported confidently, meaning nereids.

Andrula had slipped off her petticoat and was ready. She climbed on his back as she always did, but this time he advised her not to sit so tight. "I'll take you to a spot now where the water is fairly deep," he said, "but you needn't be afraid. When I tell you, take a deep breath and let yourself slide into the water. You will see, it will support you as long as there is air in your lungs. Every time you want to take a fresh breath you come up, as I do. Don't think any more about the firm ground! Leave yourself to the water and me."

He swam off with her to a small, quiet cove where the water was completely smooth and told her to stretch herself out. "Now take a deep breath!" he ordered, and slipped away from under her.

Andrula lay in the water. It really supported her, but only for a moment, because she exhaled, felt herself sinking, and beat madly around with her arms. But the dolphin was already by her side and his tail slipped under her shoulder to hold her up. Andrula could catch on to one of his fins and lift her face out of the water to get air.

"Well?" he asked her.

"Awful," answered Andrula, because she had swallowed a lot of salty seawater.

"Let's do it over again, right away!" said the dolphin. "Do you still have courage?"

"Of course," said Andrula. She took a deep breath and let go. This time she exhaled while she was stretched

out in the water. She pressed down with her arms and
kicked the water with her legs and found herself afloat.
She was able to catch another breath of air without swal-
lowing part of the Aegean Sea.

The big fish stayed close to her, never too close, but
he was always near. That gave her the confidence she
needed. She knew how swiftly he could turn. Once
more she was able to do a couple of strokes. Then she
breathed the wrong way and sank. But before she could
splutter and struggle he was beside her. He lifted her
onto his back and carried her ashore.

Breathless, laughing, and proud, Andrula pulled herself onto her rock.

"How did I do?" she asked.

"Not too badly for the first time," he commended her,
and he gave her some more instructions. Andrula, rest-
ing on the warm rock, listened attentively.

In two days she was swimming bravely next to the
dolphin, only short stretches, but without reaching for
his fin after every third stroke. Up on the cliff stood the

four fauns, watching her new game anxiously. It was only too clear that they didn't think much of it.

"Come down and learn to swim too!" Andrula shouted up to them. She tried to wave, sank, and came up again, laughing and spluttering.

The four shook their curly heads in horrified unison, turned around and raced off.

15

In the meantime Andrula's mother went every day to
Stavro's vineyard for the grape harvest. Stavro's wife
was unable to help him this year because she was ex-
pecting her fourth child. Evangelia was only too glad
to help, since it brought in some money. She would
have liked to take Andrula along, but Stavro was not
too generous. He did not want to pay for another pair
of hands.

After working in the vineyard, Evangelia would go
with Stavro to his house and help there. She was always
late coming home, and so tired that she noticed nothing
unusual about her daughter. She did not notice, for
instance, that Andrula had washed her hair again, or
that her few clothes hung so often on the bushes to
dry. Nor did she see that Andrula's skin was getting
more and more deeply tanned and that sometimes Andrula started to say something, only to bite her lip
firmly at the last moment—almost betraying herself.

For Andrula was so filled with pride over her new
achievement that she would have loved nothing better

than to run all over the island shouting to every man, woman, child, cat and dog: "I can swim! I can swim!" Of course, most of all she wanted to tell her mother, but that was impossible.

When Evangelia asked her during supper what she had done all day, Andrula answered briefly, "Just played," or "Looked for shells," or "Watched Sotiris." The fisherman often sat in front of his house in the shade, mending his nets, and the children liked to sit with him. He always had stories to tell—of the nereids, about sponge diving, the great storms and shipwrecks and miraculous rescues out at sea.

Evangelia only nodded when her daughter answered like that and did not ask any further. She saw that Andrula had done her chores faithfully. Once or twice, of course, she had left something undone and said afterwards that she had forgotten all about it. Usually it was errands or messages which had to be delivered in the Chora, but even that did not seem unusual to Evangelia. She was not even really angry. She was much too tired for that, and Andrula seemed to rebel against the slightest scolding now. That was because she had a bad conscience and she knew perfectly well that she deserved her mother's reprimand, and much more than that.

Andrula cherished every moment of her freedom. Fortunately the vineyards were on the land side of the hill and everybody was so busy that the days never seemed

long enough. And the fishermen went out during the
night. There was nobody to see Andrula slip away.

Only one thing was not as easy as it had been at
the beginning of her adventures. The vine had little
by little run out of grapes, and Andrula had none left
to take to the dolphin. Stavro's wife sometimes gave Evangelia part of their harvest, but not always. And if Evangelia did bring a bunch of grapes home at night, she
insisted that Andrula eat them right away. Andrula did
not get much to eat these days anyhow, because she
cooked nothing for herself, even when she was told to.

It won't be long now, thought Evangelia. Soon harvest
time would be over, Stavro would pay her, and the
very next Sunday Andrula should have some meat—her
favorite dish: small chunks of lamb stuck on skewers,
grilled over a slow charcoal fire and sprinkled with marjoram. The thought of such a treat and of Andrula's
delight made her mother so happy that she went quickly
to sleep that night.

She slept so soundly that she did not hear Andrula
get up from their mat and steal away.

The night was full of stars. Far out on the sea there
was a strong, bright light. Sotiris was fishing, with a
lamp to attract the fish. A dog barked in the Chora,
and farther down another one answered. Otherwise all
was still.

Andrula knew what she had to do. She had to go
to the vineyard where the grapes had been picked today.

Nobody would be watching to protect the grapevines.
A few grapes would have been forgotten by the fruit
pickers, maybe low on the vine. Not everyone liked to
bend down that far.

But she had to be very quiet and quick so that no
one would hear her and Mother wouldn't miss her.

And she was quiet, as quiet as the owl who was
just flying past her, and she was quick, too. She gathered a little pile of grapes, almost as much as a medium-
sized cluster, and she managed to hide them without
her mother waking up. But even though her task had
been completed successfully, she could not really be
happy about it. It was an unwritten law of the island
that no one took another's grapes without permission.
And even though these grapes would have dried unnoticed on the vine, Andrula had to admit to herself
that she had taken another's property.

It is for my dear dolphin, she repeated to herself over
and over again. She herself would not touch a single

grape. It was a resolve that would stand as firm as the Chora itself. "For the dolphin, for my dolphin! These are the last ones. I will never do it again," she promised herself. Yet she was unable to fall asleep for the pounding of her heart.

16

The last September days went by like spring days, clear and beautiful. These were happy days for Andrula when she spent them on Hyria. Still, now and then came days she called black even though the sun shone golden. Every day that she had to spend at home seemed to her black and ugly.

Meanwhile she had learned to dive. She brought small, delicate shells the color of a rainbow up from the bottom of the sea, or encrusted and strangely intertwined branches. These treasures she offered to the nymph Callisto, who played with them in her spring. Andrula could even dive from the rocks into the deep water, and she swam with the dolphin like one of the fifty daughters of the sea.

These pretty and heartless beings had finally realized that she was no silly human child with whom they could play until she lost her life. Andrula had not been misled even when for the hundredth time they promised her pearls and corals, mountains of pearls and corals!

Besides, the dolphin who protected her never left her side.

Life had never been so wonderful, thought the girl as she ran over the short green grass of the island. She sang out loud and danced for joy, and her playmates, the four fauns, sang and danced with her.

She had grown a lot during the last few weeks. Melas noticed it one day when she turned, dancing, under his arm.

"What is the matter with you?" he asked, astonished. "Did you stretch yourself?"

"Why?" asked Andrula carelessly, paying attention to her dance steps.

"Look!" He offered his hand and she turned under it. Sure enough, he had to reach way up to give her enough room.

"I must have grown," declared Andrula, to whom growing was nothing new.

"Grown?" asked four voices all at once. The boys forgot their dancing and crowded around her, measuring themselves against her height.

"Of course. Don't you do it?" Suddenly she realized that these fauns did not grow, just as the grass on Hyria never faded, the nightingale never flew off, and the grape hyacinths never disappeared from the fields.

Yet they had changed, too, her four companions. They were no longer quite so rough. Andrula could see it most in Melas. Wild as he was when he wrestled with his brothers, to her he was always gentle and attentive. He was a good friend, and so was Balios. Balios was by far the quickest and cleverest of the brothers. His many questions showed that he was interested about everything she had said about life in the Chora.

Even Gelanor, who had been so silly that she could not do anything with him—even this clumsy Gelanor had learned to tell right from left, and that he had to cross his feet in front when she said "front" and behind when she said "behind," not the other way around. Now she could really hope to teach them a Tsamikos they could be proud of.

And Battos! Her little Battos, who truly had a heart. He himself had discovered it and he tried to let it speak even though his tongue was heavy. But his tongue was not as heavy lately, either. Oh, Battos! Andrula smiled when she thought of him. He was the little brother she had wished for for so long.

It was Battos, too, who had first thought of fetching honey for Andrula. There really was honey on Hyria, in a cave they all knew. Wild bees lived in it. They had collected and stored honey there for centuries. Andrula liked to eat honey, and she had told Battos herself.

"She told us too," added Balios when the little one, excited and therefore less intelligible than usual, offered his plan. "I remember, we talked about how people have to eat and the different things she likes."

Balios was right. That was how the subject had come up. Andrula had noticed that when the boys were hungry they mentioned drinking.

"You mean you are thirsty," she had corrected them, but all four had stubbornly shaken their heads.

"Hungry," Melas had insisted, putting a hand on his bare brown middle. "Empty here, and tired in the head. Then we go to Callisto's Spring and she feeds us."

"And that is all you need?"

"What else should we need?"

Whereupon Andrula had told them how it was with human beings. She had named all the things she liked to eat: yoghurt from sheep's milk, and all kinds of cheese, and rock melons or the big, dark green watermelons which were pink and red inside with black or white pits. And she loved to eat young almonds (she did not mention the lamb chunks on a skewer—it would hardly have been tactful!) and nuts, and naturally, honey.

"Honey is what bees eat," the clever Balios had said.

"Yes, but we do too. We take it away from the bees

and eat it on fresh white bread." Andrula laughed, and ran her tongue over her lips in sweet memory.

That was what Battos had remembered and pondered long and hard. He did not have yoghurt from sheep's milk, whatever that might be, to please Andrula, nor melons with white or black pits, nor nuts either. But there was honey on the island.

With this important discovery Battos went to his brothers. At first they were not too enthusiastic about what he had to tell them. In fact they were rather cool.

"Bees sting," remarked Gelanor. He knew. He had sat on one once.

"S-s-s-so what?" said Battos, bold like a knight who learns that his princess is being watched by a dragon.

His brothers slowly became interested. They had not been to the cave for a long time, and they felt the urge now to nose around in its mysterious semidarkness. And since Melas, Balios and Battos had never been stung by a bee, they began to plan the adventure light-heartedly.

Gelanor did not even think of excluding himself, but he was not quite so lighthearted about it.

17

The cave lay deep in the hard, pale gray rocks which rose from one side of Hyria's other, larger hill. The boys decided to take Andrula not quite as far as this ridge of rocks. There she must stay, because she was not supposed to know what the four of them had planned. It would be a surprise. When they came back—honey! Honey for Andrula.

Andrula was very happy when the brothers told her about their plans. She still did not know any more of the island than a strip of the coast, Callisto's Spring and the little valley where she played with the fauns. It was high time she saw more of Hyria. If she had known what her four friends really had in mind! She ran after them, lightfooted and swift and completely unsuspecting in her short, faded petticoat and bare feet.

She had never realized that the island was so big, and that there were so many mighty trees. As they left the valley they came to a ravine where old plane trees grew. Callisto's Spring had become a little brook here, splashing cheerfully in the shade of the long branches.

Behind the ravine were bushes with tender green foliage, and an apple tree stood at the end of the brook, slightly bent; it was covered with pale and deep pink blossoms.

Andrula had never seen an apple tree in bloom. A little farther down the path she spied some young quince trees, six or seven of them. They also were flowering, but not as abundantly. Every blossom stood white and by itself on its stem among the downy new leaves. Below them lay small pools of dark and lighter blue—grape hyacinths.

"Aren't you coming?" called the boys, who were far ahead of her. They passed by all this beauty carelessly, but to Andrula it was like some fantastic dream. She had to tear herself away. She shook herself like a puppy who has been asleep, and ran after the four brothers.

"Is it much farther?" she asked when she reached them, out of breath.

"No, look, up there where the rocks are. That's where we want to go. But you must stay here and rest in the shade," said Melas.

"Oh, can't I go all the way up with you?" asked Andrula, very disappointed.

"Not today," explained Balios. "Next time we'll take you with us all the way to the top."

Andrula sat down on the grass and hugged her knees. She watched as her playmates went on. Quick and sure-footed, they clambered over the large rocks, and soon disappeared.

I hope they don't stay too long, thought Andrula. She picked some blades of grass and began to braid them.

But before she could think of what to do with them, she heard a pitiful screaming from the top of the hill. Four stumbling, wildly waving figures came racing down the slope, followed by a large dark cloud of angry bees.

At first Andrula did not understand why the boys were screaming and dancing, swinging their arms. They even threw themselves on the ground and rolled about! This was no game.

She ran toward them, but uphill it wasn't so easy, so she was too late to meet the bees. They had stayed with their honeycombs which, under attack, the little thieves had had to throw away.

And what a sight these honey thieves were! One of

them had been stung on eyelid and ear, another on lip
and neck, the third on nose and cheek, and they were
all beginning to swell up. Little Battos looked as if he
had the mumps. All four still rolled, moaning and groan-
ing, in the grass, trying to rid themselves of the few
bees which were still buzzing angrily in their hair and
fur.

Only Battos could offer the horrified girl a piece of
golden honeycomb, which he had saved through all this
disaster in his sting-riddled little hand—honey, wild honey
for Andrula.

She picked the last of the bees out of the boys'
hair, extracted as many stingers as she could find, and
led them all down to the spring where she applied cool-
ing compresses made from her little slip. Only when
they heard that Battos had saved a piece of honeycomb
did the fauns brighten up a little. So it had not all
been in vain.

Andrula laughed and called them "silly little goats"
and praised them lavishly—all in one breath—until the
brothers finally looked out almost proudly from their
swollen faces. Then she broke a piece off the honeycomb
and tasted it.

"Oh, that is the best honey in all Greece!" she cried
out. "There is none better even on Mount Hymettos!
Try some." And she offered the honeycomb to the
boys.

But they would only dip a fingertip into the dark,
fragrant gold which dripped from the angular cells. They

licked the honey hesitantly and shook their heads. They'd rather not get used to that taste at all.

On the evening of that memorable day, as Andrula scrambled home over the large rocks, she found a slender yellow flower bud. Was this the first fall crocus? Then soon it would be October, and school would begin; it would be the end of her freedom.

She picked the flower, and two more which had broken through a crack farther up. She was going to take them to her mother, who loved these crocuses so much. But then she remembered that her mother would ask where she had found them. No, she could not take them home. But throw them away? That would be a sin, they were so beautiful.

Finally she turned off the path and ran to the little chapel. The Blessed Virgin should have them.

Andrula put the three golden buds in front of the dark icon, but she hardly looked at it as she quickly crossed herself. Yet when her mother asked her where she had been, she said, "To the Gitonissa."

"That was right," praised Evangelia, and she smiled at Andrula.

18

The next day, when Andrula arrived particularly early on Hyria, there was not a trace of the four brothers, and she had been so worried about her little bee-stung friends.

But when she bent over Callisto's Spring to drink, it murmured from below with a gentle laughter, "They are sleeping off their pain. The poor children! I did what I could." Callisto often spoke to Andrula in this way, though she had never shown herself again after their first encounter.

"Thank you," whispered Andrula just as softly. She never dared to speak out loud here, or to tread heavily.

She went away slowly, not quite knowing what to do with herself. The dolphin, who had a hearty appetite, had swum away for a while to fish. She was all alone. The next few hours lay empty before her, waiting for her like a lovely new path. Andrula tossed the hair from her forehead. Oh well, she would let the path be her guide.

At first it took her in the direction of the ravine, and

Andrula thought she would take a look at the cave by herself. Then she remembered that the bees might still be angry and not exactly welcome a visit. She turned off on a new path leading away from the brook toward a thicket, and from the thicket to a sunny slope. And in the sun—in the sun, right in front of her was—

Andrula almost screamed out loud. A monster—half man, half horse! She stood frozen, and hardly dared breathe.

The strange beast lay there, asleep. It had not noticed her. Noiselessly she sank down on her knees behind a bush. How could she manage to get away without its hearing or seeing her?

Then she remembered that no one on Hyria could harm her because she was a guest. The thought quieted her and gave her the courage at least to look at this man-horse. It was not every day that you saw such a monster. She had often heard about him, but she didn't know that there was one on the island too. He was supposed to live in Arcadia and on Mount Pelion, a creature of the mountains and thick woods.

There, Andrula had heard, the man-horse came out of the woods at night to rattle at the doors of isolated huts. He was up to no good, that was certain. But if one had strong bolts on the windows and doors one could ward him off by leaving a large sieve outside, next to the door. He would not know what to make of it. A bowl with holes? How many holes might there be? Then the night visitor would forget why he had come. He would begin to count the holes, and that took time because he could only count to two, poor thing. He would sit in front of the door with the sieve and count: one, two—one, two—one, two—until the cock crowed. Then he would have to go back into the woods.

Oh, thought Andrula, if I only had a sieve! But she did not, and she thought she would soon find out what the monster did to people who fell into his hands.

She could not help herself. Again and again she had to look through the filigree of leaves. How big he was! His mighty horse body was reddish brown and smooth as silk, and above it were the fair chest and broad shoulders of a man. His hair and his long tail were a shade darker.

He was sound asleep. Could she still slip away before he woke up? Just as she was deciding to try it, he sneezed heartily. Andrula ducked back behind her bush.

Now he stretched, opened his arms wide, and yawned. Then he jumped up on his four feet. He was even bigger than Andrula had thought. A gasp of surprise escaped her. She bit her knuckles, but it was too late. He had heard it. At once he came over to the bush that hid her, bent down and picked her out of it as easily as one picks up a hat or a small bundle.

"You can see me better close by, Echo!" he said. He held her off with outstretched arms and laughed.

Andrula managed to answer. "I'm not Echo. My name is Andrula," she stammered, lips trembling. But she looked bravely into his eyes.

"I am glad to meet you, Andrula," said the man-horse, putting her down on the rock he had been leaning against and shaking her hand heartily. "I am not Narcissus either, but Aglaos. But if one is being watched by an eavesdropping little nymph through the bushes— why are you so afraid of me?"

"Because you are a monster," answered Andrula frankly.

"I? A monster? Whatever gave you that idea? What does it mean, anyhow?"

"Oh, something dreadful! It comes out of the woods at night and rattles at the door and steals people and it is also very stupid," explained Andrula thoughtlessly.

"And that is what you think of me?" said Aglaos. He straightened himself to his full height and spread his arms wide. "Look at me! Do I look dreadful? I, Aglaos the Centaur? Do you know what my name means?"

Andrula shook her head.

"The Magnificent," said Aglaos simply. He folded his arms across his wide chest and enjoyed her confusion.

Andrula sat on the rock and wished for nothing so much as a mousehole—and that she'd be small enough to crawl into it.

He laughed out loud and picked her up, swung her around onto his strong back and took off at full speed over the sunny slopes, then on through the shady forest. His four hoofs thundered. As he galloped along he let out high, triumphant cries. But once in the forest he slowed his speed and reached for low-hanging branches to bend them gently out of the way.

At first Andrula grabbed his flying mane with both hands. He went so fast that she could hardly breathe.

Her hair flew, her face glowed. She had never ridden anything faster than Stavro's little donkey, and to compare this centaur ride with a donkey ride was laughable. She might as well have compared the ride on the dolphin with the one in Sotiris' old boat. But soon she found herself rejoicing along with Aglaos, and when they turned into the forest she even dared to take one hand off his mane and pat his shoulder softly—the horse shoulder. He turned around and laughed at her happily, showing his white, shining teeth.

Then he took her slowly uphill through the woods, under sweet chestnut trees and mighty pines. How big was this island? It was no hill they were climbing, it was a mountain! On top there were wide open stretches and Aglaos sped across them, light and free as the wind. Above them was only the sky with round white clouds. Andrula laughed and sang.

Little by little she seemed to recognize things—those rocks, the valley over there. Aglaos stopped. From this high point they could see the sea. It was dark blue, with many whitecaps.

"You will not have such a smooth ride home today, little Andrula," said the centaur. "Run along now, and have a happy trip! Are you coming back tomorrow?"

"Yes," promised Andrula quickly. "But we mustn't go so far, you know. I have to take care of my little fauns. They are bound to be well by then, don't you think so?"

Aglaos laughed. Andrula told him of the four brothers and their adventure with the bees. She had told him everything—about the Chora, and cousin Stassa, about her mother who was always so quiet, and her father who had been lost at sea, and even that she had stolen grapes for the dolphin. This strong, beautiful Aglaos had quickly become as familiar to her as an old and trusted friend.

She told the dolphin about her day as they rode homeward through the foaming whitecaps. "I had no idea that the island was so large! It is much larger than Kalonysos and Ryos put together."

"Oh Andrula," said the dolphin, "haven't you noticed that Hyria is to everyone whatever he needs? For the fauns it is a green valley; for Aglaos it is mountains—"

And for me . . . thought Andrula, but she did not say what Hyria was for her. She could not find a word that was good and big enough. But her dolphin understood, even without words.

19

Andrula could not keep the promise which she had so hastily made to Aglaos. The next day was the first of October, and the beginning of school.

Evangelia combed her daughter's hair, tied a fresh apron around her waist, gave her the woven satchel which served as a school bag, and kissed her good-bye. Andrula let everything happen to her as if she were made of wood. Her eyes were as dark as windows without light.

"What is the matter, Andrula?" asked her mother, worried. "You are not going to be ill, are you?" And she quickly felt her forehead. It was quite cool.

"I don't want to go to school," said Andrula.

"But you have always liked to go!" said her mother, surprised. "What are you talking about? Go, my little love, go, or you'll be late."

Sullenly and slowly Andrula went through the door. If Evangelia hadn't already had her thoughts on her weaving she could have seen, from the small back and drooping shoulders, how reluctantly Andrula began her walk to school. But this morning Evangelia had to string the main threads for a runner, a tedious job with which Theano, the potter's wife, had offered to help her. So now she hurried to have everything ready, and she forgot to wave to Andrula.

Andrula stopped for a moment at the place where the path to the beach turned off. She considered whether she shouldn't just slip away as she had done so often. But before, nobody but old Katsika knew about it. This time there was a school full of children and teachers waiting in the village, and everybody would know that she was missing on the first day after vacation. She could not risk it, not today.

Slowly she walked on. The satchel in her hand was heavy as lead and her heart was even heavier. Up in the Chora doors were opening and other children came out and tried to join her. But Andrula looked at them with hostility and ran ahead. She was one of the first to arrive.

It was just like it had always been in the schoolyard. The big boys stood together in one group and tried to talk like men. The big girls greeted each other loudly as if they hadn't seen each other for weeks. The little ones chased each other this way and that all around the yard like loud, shrill swallows.

Andrula belonged to the not-so-small but not-yet-big ones, but she joined neither group. She stayed close to the door and pretended to be looking for something in her satchel. Fortunately the teacher, Mr. Sophoklis, came out of his house next to the school. He crossed the yard with quick steps, answering the greetings of the children: "Good morning, Andromache! Stelio, good morning! Good morning, all of you!"

Miss Aliki, the teacher of the lower grades, came running too, holding a new pupil by the hand. The child was afraid of being late the first day of school.

Two of the big boys jumped toward the old olive tree where the school bell hung and began ringing it as hard as they could. There were no latecomers, however, not today.

School began.

First Mr. Sophoklis welcomed them all once again. Then he said a prayer. Not one of the children dared glance at his neighbor or at the stack of new books on the teacher's desk. Mr. Sophoklis was very strict and kept them under close discipline.

Then they were given permission to sit down, the little ones in front and the littlest ones on the floor, for they too were assembled in the "big" classroom. Miss Aliki sat on a chair at the end of their row, her hands folded. All the children were very attentive, for the teacher was now making a speech. He always made a speech the last day before vacation as well as the first day of school, and he always said the same things: that the children were now, in God's name, beginning their studies, and that he was quite sure that they had the best intentions, and that he hoped this good will would last longer than the first few days. (Here the children were permitted to laugh, but only briefly.) It was now up to them whether this would be a fruitful year for them or not.

Then Mr. Sophoklis changed his ceremonious tone, and divided different tasks among the bigger children. Ringing the school bell: that rotated. Collecting the books: that was a weekly chore. Taking care of the needlework closet: Maria and big Sophia. Blackboard and chalk box: Jorgakis. And on and on.

Andrula had hardly listened during the speech, but when the duties were assigned, she paid close attention. The list was finished at last and her heart fell back into place with such relief that she was sure her neighbors must have heard it. What if they had given her even one small job! It might have been for a whole month—like Stassa, for instance, who had to water the potted plants and now sat there beaming, proud as a peacock. Never had Andrula envied her less.

But Stassa, who had noticed Andrula's deep sigh of relief, thought she had sighed out of envy, and puffed herself up twice as big. She had a job, the only one of the middle group! And Andrula had none, not even a little one. Andrula was no more than a fly on the wall.

A little later, Stassa's smile became even more superior. The little children had left the room with Miss Aliki, and the lessons for the bigger ones began. The teacher, who always tried to make the first day of school as pleasant as possible, started with the old Greek myths. First he asked questions to see how much they still remembered. These were short and easy questions, but now he was asking for the third time: "Andrula?

Andrula! Name the twelve labors of Herakles. Andrula!"

Andrula came to with a jerk, and it was only too clear that she had not heard a word, except for her name. She stood, as if torn out of the deepest sleep, and the whole class giggled.

Mr. Sophoklis did not know what to make of it. He had always considered Andrula one of his brightest pupils, and now, so dreamy, so inattentive! Ah well, these overlong summer vacations—they buried everything that he tried so hard to plant into these young heads.

He reprimanded Andrula for her absentmindedness and went on: "The next one—you, little Sophia!"

And Sophia rattled off the labors of Herakles as smoothly as clockwork, and just as thoughtlessly.

Andrula tried to follow the lesson, but without success. Again and again her thoughts flew to Hyria. Had the bee stings of the four brothers healed? Was Aglaos looking for her? And her dear dolphin! How he must be waiting, swimming back and forth in the little cove!

She seemed to hear the resounding voice of the man-horse as he stormed across the slopes, and the happy shouts of the fauns, and then again the quiet whisper of the spring: "Lovely, lovely shells, Andrula! Drink, drink, good health, Andrula." Silver around the edges of the shells, silver on colored pebbles, soft laughter. "Come back, Andrula. Come back soon!"

The voice of the teacher was now hard and angry: "How many times do I have to call you, Andrula?"

Andrula had to stand in the corner, and Stassa jeered.

20

The first rain of autumn fell and refreshed the arid fields. Everyone was relieved because the rain had taken its time. Summer had been unusually long and the water in the wells had sunk dangerously low.

The people of the Chora, too, felt refreshed when the large drops fell, first slowly, one by one, then in a heavy shower. The girls sang in the courtyards; up in the church the bell rang.

Andrula was the only one who was not glad. She had not been to her island for three days and the day after tomorrow was Sunday. That only left Saturday, because she could not bear to wait until Monday.

Should she go tomorrow? She might go to school as usual and try to slip away unnoticed after the bell rang. The dolphin knew that school had started again. She had run down to the cove quickly after the first day of school and told him. Her poor friend! He had waited for her all these hours. He had offered to wait for her every day just in case she could get away.

Andrula had been scolded and punished often during

these three days, but it did not help. She just could not follow the teacher's words. Again and again her thoughts flew away, like birds that fly home, home to the island of Hyria.

Nor could she bring herself to play with her classmates. It was as if a deep water separated her from all the other children. Andrula could see them as on a far shore, but she was unable to cross over. The water was too deep. They were strangers. Some of them were even enemies, Stassa and two or three others. They plagued and teased Andrula whenever they could, and gloated openly when she was punished.

On Hyria there was no gloating. If one of the boys tripped over the other and all of them laughed about that, there was no malice in it. There were no pointed remarks, no sly looks, no secret whisperings in the corner, and no giggling behind anybody's back!

Andrula had never been so unhappy. She did not know how she could stand it. The worst was the homesickness. She would even have embraced one of the nereids like a sister after these endless three days. The nereids were sometimes unkind too, but you could not hold it against them, because they had no heart. But these children here who tormented her, they had hearts. They should have known better.

The weather was still sunny and mild. With some luck it might stay warm until the middle of November; Andrula would be able to ride over to the island until then. And she firmly intended to as often and as long as possible. Later, of course, when the great winter storms came and the sea was cold as ice— But Andrula did not even want to think about that. Then she would be completely trapped.

Andrula managed on this first Saturday in October to slip away unnoticed before school began. She took the little steep path down to the beach. It was quite simple. Nobody was near the coast at this early hour.

But now the whole shoreline lay ahead of her, empty and completely without protection. Reaching the other end without being seen seemed almost impossible. Any moment someone might appear. The people who lived in the huts nearby were always doing something at the water's edge. Andrula could only trust to luck, and sure enough, it was with her today. Quick as a lizard she slipped across the bright sand. Never before had she arrived at the little cove so out of breath. Her heart beat so fast she could hardly greet the dolphin.

He was there, of course. And he was beside himself with happiness to have his little friend back again. He swished through the water as only a dolphin can. He dived, he leaped, he shot to and fro, turned like a flash until the water in the little cove churned wildly. Andrula, who had been breathless with excitement and hurry, was now breathless with laughter. Then she sat on his back and they were off to Hyria, like an arrow, straight ahead.

Forty-four nereids swam out to greet them, laughing and singing, white garlands in their hands. Andrula was escorted to the island in triumph. Today she could even dare to swim with the nereids—close to the shore and under the watchful eye of the dolphin, of course. This time there were no thoughtless tricks in their beautiful fair heads. They called Andrula "little sister" and adorned her head and neck with fantastic wreaths made of seaweed, shells and tiny starfish, and on her ears they fastened little shrimp as earrings. They put a twisted pink-encrusted twig into her hand and played "You Are Our Queen" with her.

Suddenly in the midst of all this fun came a bleating and trumpeting from the cliffs above. Andrula looked up. There stood her four playmates blowing into their hands the way tritons blow into sea shells, and bleating like little goats in the stable who want to go out into the sun. All this was aimed at Andrula and clearly meant, "Come up, come up! Aren't you coming soon?"

She freed herself at once from the circle of nereids and swam to shore. But first she had to kneel down at the spring and offer the ornaments from her hair. The shrimps were not there anymore—they had let go before she came out of the water—but everything else was for Callisto: seaweed and shells and the pointed starfish.

And there, where the water rippled and formed rings she appeared again, white and slender. She smiled and waved, shimmered and disappeared—Callisto herself.

Now Andrula danced twice as happily with the little fauns. Aglaos came too, stretched out in the sun and watched them. After a few minutes he trotted off, to return with a flute, a shepherd's pipe made of reeds, which he played to accompany them. They had never danced so well!

21

About ten days later the teacher's wife came to see Evangelia, to order heavier sheets for the winter. At first she talked about that, but soon changed the subject.

"How is your Andrula?" she asked, as if in passing. "What is wrong with her?"

"Andrula?" asked Evangelia, surprised. "Nothing is wrong with her!"

"What?" said Mrs. Sophoklis. "There is nothing wrong with her? Isn't she sick?"

"No," answered Evangelia, who did not understand where the lady had gotten such an idea.

"You really mustn't keep her home so often," said Mrs. Sophoklis reproachfully. "The child must go to school."

"But that is where she is!" said Evangelia, much disturbed.

"That is just where she is not," said the lady sternly. "Andrula has been to school only once in the past ten days."

With that she went out, leaving Evangelia completely

confused. She tried to continue weaving but her hands were so unsteady that she lost the shuttle several times, and finally gave up. She buried her face in her hands and thought, where is my child?

"I have let her go where she wanted to go," she spoke out loud to herself after she had been sitting for a long time. She could not stand it any longer. She had to confide her troubles to someone. She needed help in a hurry.

Evangelia jumped up and ran out of the courtyard, across the path, to the Virgin in the Fields. There, in the cool, peaceful little room, in front of the dark and golden icon, she poured out her heart. Everything rushed out: the old hurt about Andreas, her husband, who would have been such a good father for Andrula, and the bitter guilt that she herself had failed and not guided her child properly, because she was so poor, because she had to work so much and so hard. That was the reason—the only reason—why she had neglected her duty and left the girl to herself.

"But you know, Most Holy Mother, you know that it has been necessary, don't you? How else could we have lived? Tell me what I have done wrong! I implore you from the bottom of my heart."

Tears streamed over her pale face, and she sat for a long time in the darkness, weeping. Then she rose, kissed the image of the Virgin and slowly left the chapel. She felt completely drained and so exhausted that she could hardly lift her feet. She sat down for a moment,

her back against the white wall, and immediately fell asleep.

Andrula, in the meantime, was flying across the sunny slopes on Aglaos' back. He had taken her to the cave where the bees lived.

She had walked in alone, for the entrance was too narrow for her friend. She had looked up at the ceiling with amazement. The cave was shaped like a beehive, filled with the humming and buzzing of the bees that lived in it. The floor was smooth here and uneven there, and strangely shaped rocks were everywhere. From the walls hung curtains of stone and in the folds were the brown honeycombs. The honey smelled sweet and slightly fermented, because the bees collected much more pollen than they could use. The cave was a veritable storehouse of honey.

Aglaos called Andrula and she hurried back to him. She had to think of her ride home. It was very important now to time her return with the closing of school.

She talked for a while with the four boys, who had declined another excursion to the cave, and she drank from Callisto's Spring. Then she climbed onto the dolphin. It only seemed a moment before he set her down again in the small cove.

Often as Andrula had left from and returned to this spot, she had never met a human soul, not in all these weeks. But today, as she slipped on her dress, still talking happily with the dolphin, she suddenly saw someone coming down the steep hill. It was an old woman, dressed all in black, and she was heading straight toward her. Frightened, Andrula looked at her. She thought of running away, but it was too late.

Andrula knew all the old women of the village, but this woman was a total stranger to her. Maybe she had come over from the harbor to visit in the Chora. But what was she doing here, at this deserted spot?

The stranger was right in front of her now, and she looked stern and angry. She seemed to know Andrula well.

"So," she said, "this is where I find you!" She turned
to the dolphin, who had apparently also been unable
to get away. "And you," she continued, "what are you
doing with this girl? I know where you have been taking
her all these days, and I tell you, she does not belong
there. Stay in your domain! The girl belongs to this
world, and to me. Now go, and don't come back here
again!"

The dolphin behaved like a scolded boy who does
not want to show his shame. He did some of his best
leaps, but then he shot off and quickly disappeared.

Andrula stood petrified. There was something terrible,

something frightening about this strange woman who now turned to her and commanded:

"You too, go home now! I forbid you ever to come back here. From now on you will be a good daughter to your mother."

With that she turned away, and when Andrula dared raise her eyes she was already climbing up the hill. Andrula was still trembling from fright. Helplessly she sank down on the rock and looked after the dark figure disappearing over the hill.

Who was this stern woman, and what was it that had been so strange about her? She had looked like all old women in her black dress with the long, full skirt. A black scarf had been drawn tightly around her hair and chin. The pale face with its wrinkles and furrows— there were many such old women—but what was it that was so different about her?

Suddenly it came to Andrula. The feet! The stranger had been barefoot. None of the old women of the village were. Even the poorest of them wore shoes, though maybe coarse and worn out ones. But that was not all. Not only were the feet of the stranger unshod—there had not been a trace of dust on her bare feet. Yet she must have come across the dusty path of the fields and then down the rocky hill.

Andrula screamed aloud and ran home, driven by unspeakable fear.

About that time, Evangelia woke from her deep sleep at the wall of the chapel. She felt refreshed and strengthened and completely calm. Strangely, not one of all the wild thoughts which had troubled her heart seemed to remain. Her mind was as if swept clean. Only a few words lingered on, a line of a song she had often sung:

"And the black clothes don't look well on her . . ."

She looked down at herself as she got up, shaking out her skirt, wondering. The song was right! She was still young, only twenty-eight years old, much too young for the black clothes she had put on when she was eighteen.

She herself had done wrong, not Andrula. If a child no longer had a father, she still had a right to a mother who could be young and happy with her. Evangelia saw it quite clearly now, and she promised herself and the Gitonissa to be such a mother for Andrula from now on.

The little girl was already coming toward her. How strange she looked!

Andrula had taken the shortest way home. But she had found yard and house empty, and she needed her mother now, this very moment. And so she ran out of the door again, along the path, and there she found her mother. She ran to her and threw her arms around her. "Manula, Manula."

"There, there, my little bird," said Evangelia tenderly. "Hush, I am here."

And Andrula quieted down. Her terrible fear subsided. She slipped her fingers into the cool, firm hand of her mother and walked home with her.

They were both quiet. Even later, when they lay in the dark room, Evangelia only said, "I don't want to plague you with questions, Andrula. I don't want to know where you have been and what you have been doing. I am sure that it could not have been anything bad."

"No, it was nothing bad," murmured Andrula, all scrubbed and clean between fresh sheets. "I did nothing but dance and play, and I learned how to swim."

"For goodness' sake!" cried her mother in dismay. "And I have always told you not to go near the water!"

But she did not want to scold. She wanted to start anew. She knew now what Andrula had been doing instead of going to school. Somehow she had learned to swim, and then she had not wanted to do anything else but swim. That explained everything. She silently promised the Gitonissa a candle, because a great danger had passed by Andrula.

22

The next day Andrula went back to school, obedient and docile.

Mr. Sophoklis noticed her as soon as he stepped into the schoolyard, and he called her over. "Oh, Andrula, have you been ill?"

"No," she answered, because there were to be no more lies and subterfuge.

"So?" said the teacher thoughtfully. "Then why didn't you come to school?"

"I wanted to be outdoors."

"Yes, who doesn't want that," agreed Mr. Sophoklis. "But when you reach a certain age all that is over, at least between vacations! Have you been punished?"

Andrula lowered her head. "Yes," she whispered.

"Then let us forget it," declared the teacher with a friendly nod, and he entered the schoolhouse.

The same morning Evangelia, too, went into the village—to Mitso, the merchant, to look at material for a dress.

"For yourself, Vangelio?" asked Mitso, who had gone to school with her. "You want black." He reached for a black bale. Evangelia blushed deeply.

"Yes, for me, Mitso," she said. "But please, something a little brighter this time, not black."

"That's what I like to hear," said Mitso. "Look here. I have just the right thing for you." He brought out a pretty black and white checked piece of fabric and put it in front of her.

Evangelia liked it. "But it is probably expensive, Mitso," she said. "You know—"

"Of course, of course," soothed the merchant as he quickly tore off the price tag. "I know. But this is not as expensive as all that. And look, here is a little flaw, and it is a remnant. If you take the whole piece you'll be doing me a favor. I'll make you a good price."

Evangelia thought about it. "I really should think about the winter," she murmured undecidedly.

"Oh, it's not coming this year," said Mitso, laughing. "I am still selling summer fabrics."

"All right, I'll take it," declared Evangelia, and a new joy radiated from her pale face as she paid for it. "My first bright dress in ten years, Mitso!" she said.

"Wear it in good health," offered the shopkeeper, and he gave her the little package.

She walked up the road to Artemisoula, the seamstress, who was called Soula for short—a cheerful, round, and talkative woman. She clapped her hands in delight. "What do I see? Vangelio! And with such a nice, bright piece of cloth! But there is much too much for Andrula," she added professionally, as she opened the paper wrapping.

"It is to be a dress for me, Soula," explained Evangelia, blushing again.

"I am glad," exclaimed Soula. She measured the fabric against her arm and calculated quickly. "It is enough for a dress and a jacket," she said.

Evangelia thought for a moment.

"No," she said. "If there is that much left over, could you make something for Andrula?"

"Is yours to be a dress with short sleeves?"

"Yes, with short sleeves."

"What a pity! It would be so fashionable with a jacket," mourned Soula. "But whatever you say. There will be enough for a skirt for Andrula."

And so they left it. Soula grew cheerful again and suggested she add a piece of red trim to Andrula's skirt. "It won't cost you anything," she promised eagerly. "I have no other use for it, and it would look so pretty."

Evangelia accepted the offer gratefully, and then she asked for Soula's price.

"I won't take anything for making Andrula's skirt," answered Soula, who was a generous woman. "And for your dress, let me see, for that you could weave me a rug. All right?"

"How good you are, Soula," said Evangelia smiling.

"Good? Me? Not at all," cried Soula. "I'm so glad you want to get out of your everlasting black."

"Could you finish both for the Feast of Saint Dimitrios, Soula?" asked Evangelia.

"Now don't tell me you are planning to go to it!" exclaimed the seamstress.

"Yes, I have stayed away from everything too long," said Evangelia softly.

"You have lived like a nun," agreed Soula briskly. "Of course you may have both things for the holiday, and I myself will go with you to hear everyone admire you in your new dress!"

On the day of the Feast of Saint Dimitrios, every able-bodied person went out to an old monastery, about an hour and a half from the Chora, where the celebrations took place. It was a beautiful spot, with a famous spring of sweet water and a garden around the church. The people of Kalonysos spread out in front of it. A whole sheep was roasted on a spit above a charcoal fire, and wine jugs made the rounds. There was eating and drinking, singing and dancing. Everyone slept through the afternoon under the trees; then there was more dancing in the evening, and far into the night.

Andrula had never been at the monastery. Actually, this was the first big festival she had ever attended. She looked wide-eyed at the lively, noisy throng and pressed herself close to her mother, who stayed on the edge of it all. Andrula was filled with an immense pride. She and her mother were both at a festival in beautiful, new clothes! She felt a pleat of her skirt. Cloth from the store! Just as good as Stassa's dress with the roses. No, better. Andrula had always thought those roses were a trifle too loud.

The young men danced in the open square in front of the monastery gate to the lively sounds of two fiddles and a guitar. Now a row of girls formed, and they debated who was to lead them.

Soula came running. "Vangelio, they want you! You used to be one of the best dancers!"

But Evangelia shook her head. She did not want to. She just could not bring herself to dance.

They left her alone as the music began again. A tall, slender man led the long chain of girls and younger women. Andrula did not know who he was, but he danced very well, and she moved a little closer in order to see better. Yes, he was a stranger, but there were many strangers here for the holiday. Two boats had come over from Ryos and Anti-Ryos.

Evangelia stayed alone, sitting on the low wall. The dance ended, and the leader turned to a group of older men. He did not stay long, but left them and came toward Evangelia. The man greeted her politely and asked if he might sit down. Evangelia nodded, somewhat surprised.

"Aren't you Andreas' wife?" he began.

"His widow," she answered.

"Yes, I know," said the stranger. "I knew Andreas well."

"Then you are a sponge diver?" asked Evangelia shyly.

"No, I only went along for the adventure, and only once." And he explained that he had been a sailor and

had sailed for several years between America and Genoa. But all that was behind him now, because his parents were old and ailing and they needed their son at home.

"Are you visiting on Kalonysos?" asked Evangelia. She liked the stranger. He spoke so quietly and frankly. And he had been Andreas' friend.

"Actually I'm here on business," he answered. "My mother owns some land on Kalonysos which she wants to sell. That is why I'm here. My name is Kosta," he added, "and my home is on Samos."

Andrula came back. She leaned against her mother and looked curiously at the stranger.

"This is Andreas' daughter," said Evangelia.

"She looks very much like her father," said Kosta. He shook Andrula's hand and said good night. He had to return to his hosts.

Shortly after that Evangelia and Andrula left too, because there was no transportation and it was a long way back to the Chora.

23

Andrula soon saw Kosta again. He was sitting with some other men in front of the coffeehouse, and he greeted her as she passed. But she forgot him right away. What was the stranger to her? She was much too busy with her own thoughts, with her misery over all that she had lost.

She had been led back to the road of duty, but she could not forget the happiness she had lost. She thought about Hyria, every hour.

She also continued to avoid the other children. It was too hard to get used to them again. Even the festival and her new dress had been a poor consolation, soon to disappear.

She tried hard at school. She was obedient at home. But she was no longer the old Andrula, who tossed her hair back in a lively way and was always full of ideas. Evangelia was worried about her quiet, depressed manner.

While the other children played after school in the village square, Andrula would sit on one of the rocks down at the beach, where the steep little path ended. She would look toward the two neighboring islands: behind them was Hyria. But she could not see the slightest bit of it from here.

One day a small boat passed by, right in front of her. The stranger, Kosta, was in it, and he waved.

"Would you like to come along?" he called over to her.

"Where to?" asked Andrula shyly.

"Oh, just for a little ride," he answered.

Andrula had stood up, but she still hesitated.

"Come on," he said in a friendly tone. "Your mother's given permission."

Surprised, Andrula let herself be helped into the boat. Kosta came about and headed for the open sea.

"I have a better boat at home, on Samos," he remarked. "But this one is better than no boat at all, don't you think so? Do you like the sea?"

"Oh yes, very much!" said Andrula. She trusted him. "When I grow up I am going to be a sailor."

He did not laugh at her. He even nodded.

"But everybody thinks a girl can't be a sailor," she added dejectedly.

"That is right," said Kosta. "But a girl can still go to sea." And he told her about the large passenger ships which hired many women: stewardesses and nurses and nursery school teachers.

"Nursery school teachers," repeated Andrula dreamily. She made him explain to her what they had to do.

"That's what I want to be," she decided quickly. "Will you help me with it, Kosta?"

"Of course I will," he promised in his quiet, sensible way. "But you still have plenty of time."

For a while they did not say anything, but enjoyed the fast ride. A fresh breeze filled the sail and the little craft skimmed lightly across the water. It grew chilly and Kosta threw a warm jacket toward Andrula.

"You know, Andrula," he said, looking at her thoughtfully, "you really should have a father like other children. Would you like that?"

"Yes," answered Andrula. "But how? My father died."

"Sometimes little girls like you can have a new father," continued Kosta. "Have you ever thought of that?"

"No," she said quietly.

"Then think about it now," suggested Kosta. And he asked, "If you could choose a father, what would he have to be like?"

"Oh, he'd have to be tall and handsome, and brave and strong," said Andrula enthusiastically. "And he'd have to have a boat and take me with him always when he sailed, even at night."

Kosta didn't say anything for a while. He had to furl the sail. Then he started the motor, because it had gotten late. Finally he said, "How about me, Andrula?"

"You?"

"Yes, I'd be tall enough, though I'm not exactly handsome," he said. "And I even have a boat. Now, what do you say?"

"Do you mean you would like to be my father?"

"That is what I mean."

"Really?"

"Really."

Andrula thought for a while. "That would be all right with me," she answered slowly. "Only, what would my mother think about it? Have you told her yet?"

"No, I have not talked to her yet."

"Do you know what, Kosta? If you want me to I could talk to her."

Kosta answered with a straight face, "Thank you, Andrula. That would be very kind of you."

But by the time they got closer to the jetty below the Chora he had changed his mind.

"I think I'd better talk to her myself, Andrula."

"Yes, maybe you are right," she agreed. She jumped lightly onto the shore and held out her hand. "Thank you for the ride, Kosta! Good night."

"Take care of yourself, Andrula," he said. And only after she had left did he smile.

The next morning, as Kosta sat opposite Evangelia in her little house, she said seriously, "A penniless widow with a child, Kosta? Your parents would never permit it."

"I have given up a lot for my parents," he replied. "They will welcome the woman I bring to them."

"Will they?" asked Evangelia doubtfully. "And then, there's Andrula. What will Andrula say?"

"She has already said it," said Kosta, suddenly very

cheerful. "She even offered to do the talking for me on this delicate subject!"

Evangelia gave him her hand. "She needs a father," she said. "I think you will be a good father to her."

24

A new dress, even a new father and the prospect of a new home were not enough to make Andrula's feet light again. She was burdened by something which she had to think out for herself. It was like a puzzle, and she had to find the solution.

No one could help her—not her mother, not even Kosta, clever as he was. There was one who could help, only she would not do it. The Gitonissa. It was she who had given her the problem to solve. Sometimes Andrula had a strong feeling that she was expected at the small chapel in the field—with the solution. And she did not even know what the problem was.

Everybody in the Chora had been very friendly since her mother's life and hers had changed for the better, but the only one to whom Andrula felt drawn was the old fisherman Sotiris. He talked of things other than the wedding, the subject which was on everyone else's mind. He spoke to her of the sea, of islands, of distant shores. He told her of adventures, of squids, mermaids, corals, and pearls. Andrula often sat with him, always hoping that he would talk, just by chance, about Hyria.

One day he did. "The island, the third one, you know, far behind Ryos and Anti-Ryos, the one that does not want us—"

"Yes?" said Andrula almost inaudibly, and her heart began to pound.

"There were people here from Ryos. Do you know what they call it? The Beehive."

"Oh," cried Andrula, forgetting herself. "The Beehive! The people from Ryos call it that too?"

The old fisherman gave her a sharp look from under his white eyebrows. "Too?" he asked dryly.

"Yes, of course." Andrula nodded eagerly. "Hyria means beehive, in the old language—"

Just to be able to say the beloved name out loud was happiness. Andrula's eyes shone. She raised her dark head quickly. She saw the surprise in Sotiris' face, and ended her sentence lamely, "—so I've heard."

"Hyria," repeated the old man thoughtfully. "And who calls the island that, in the old language?"

"People," began Andrula. But then she stopped, disturbed, and tried to avoid an answer. What would Sotiris think?

"People who know," she said finally. "But I have to go home now." She jumped up and shook out her skirt.

"Funny," murmured the old man as if he had not heard her. "Funny. Beehive—Hyria—both mean the same thing. I wonder if there is honey there, on the island."

Andrula suddenly saw the four fauns rolling in the grass, whimpering, crying, chased by hundreds of furious bees. Her face was mischievous as a pixie's. "Why don't you sail over and look for yourself?"

And like a little bird she darted away.

This talk with the old fisherman had helped her. It was the first time she had been able to say the name Hyria out loud, and it had freed something in her. Suddenly she felt much lighter.

That evening Andrula lay in bed—her mother was still sitting at the loom, though she weaved things only for herself now—and she stared up at the crooked beam of the ceiling. She thought everything through until it came crystal clear.

Part of me has stayed in Hyria, she thought. That much is certain. Something else is just as certain, that part of Hyria has stayed with me. That can never be changed, and that is what I have to tell the Gitonissa, whether she wants to hear it or not. Holy Mother, I will tell her—and with that Andrula's eyes closed. Whatever it was she had intended to tell the Holy Mother was held in safekeeping by sleep.

Several days later she heard something, from Sotiris and the other fishermen, that only confirmed her decision. They were talking about a dolphin who had appeared recently, every time a boat went out. Dolphins were never very shy, said the fishermen, but this one! He would come very close to the boat and leap up again and again, almost as if he wanted to see who was in it. They had given him a name. "The nosey one" they called him.

Soon almost the whole Chora was talking about the unusual behavior of this dolphin, and they argued back and forth about whether his appearance was a good omen or not. The school children embellished the story, until newer things came along to talk about.

Andrula had listened to all the talk but had known better than to say anything. She was quite sure that their curious dolphin was none other than her friend, and she also knew what he was looking for in the boats. Not what—whom.

Now she *must* go to the chapel in the field, as soon

as possible. If there were only something she could take to the Gitonissa!

She got up her courage and went to the teacher's wife.

"Please, Mrs. Sophoklis," she asked, "do you have anything I could do for a drachma?"

The lady smiled and said that she well might have. "But what do you need the money for, Andrula?"

Andrula answered truthfully. "For a candle I want to light before the Gitonissa."

"Then come along," said Mrs. Sophoklis and she went ahead of Andrula into the house to the kitchen. "Katinitsa has a toothache. Look, she left me with all the dishes. I was just about to do them myself. But if you want to do them for me, I'll give you a drachma, no, two."

Andrula began her work immediately, thinking to herself that she really should not take any money for it. It was so exciting just to see all the things in this kitchen and in the cupboards! At first she refused to accept the second drachma, but Mrs. Sophoklis was practical as well as pious. "The candles for two drachmas are thicker, Andrula!"

It flashed through Andrula's mind that One who walked with bare feet through the dust without being touched by it could expect a two-drachma candle. She took her pay and the caramel which was given to her as well, and ran home.

"Manula," Andrula called from the door, almost her old lively self. "I did a job for Mrs. Sophoklis, and she gave me money for it. May I go to the Gitonissa and light a candle?"

"Yes, certainly," answered Evangelia. "But wait until evening. Then I'll come with you."

"No, Manula, please! I have to go alone," Andrula begged.

"Then go," said her mother.

Andrula went down the path which she had carefully avoided ever since the day of her last hasty visit to the chapel, a day she had tried to forget.

She stood in the little room where the dusk had already fallen, put her candle—how imposing two-drachma candles were!—into the holder which was filled with sand, fetched matches from the nook and lit the candle. The light shone straight at the old icon.

Andrula stood in front of it, her hands at her back. She looked up and into the eyes of the Gitonissa.

"Mother believes you are here," she said softly. "But I think you are everywhere. Anyhow, here is where you listened to Mother, and this is your house, so I've come to speak to you here."

There was no reply, and Andrula went on. "I don't want to disobey, but you have to realize something too. Those over there on Hyria are my friends. I can't just leave them without a word. They are talking in the Chora about a dolphin who swims up and down the shore. He is looking for me. I am not going to go to him, because you forbade me to do it. But if he finds me, I will talk to him."

Andrula's voice had become quite loud at the end,

and it seemed to her that the little chapel was filled with her words. But the stillness returned and nothing happened. She listened inwardly.

Something in her said, "You are daring, Andrula."

She answered back immediately. "Would you rather have me timid and weak and unfaithful?"

Nothing else came. She waited for a while. Then she began to laugh, and she looked for an answering smile in the large, dark eyes in the picture. She thought she saw it. Or was it the flicker of her candle?

"No," said Andrula with conviction. "You would rather have me bold." Only then did she take the last step toward the icon and kiss the fine wrist below the golden sleeve band.

25

The wedding was to be celebrated on Samos, because Kosta's mother was too weak to travel to Kalonysos. Kosta had settled his business affairs and had left Kalonysos to get everything at home ready for the arrival of Evangelia and Andrula.

Someone was found to rent the little house above the beach. Evangelia and Andrula packed, and then they had to say good-bye to everyone in the Chora. That was the custom. Everyone praised Evangelia's good fortune and wished them well in their new life. Even Aunt Stamatina and Stassa seemed filled with kindness. And if they didn't really mean it, those two, well, that was their business. Evangelia wanted to leave her home in peace, and Andrula agreed with her.

Andrula was happy to leave. It would be good to begin again, to meet new people and see new things. Kosta had told her about Samos, about the tall mountains and deep woods and how beautiful his home was. The terraced vineyards went all the way down to the sea, he said, and nowhere were figs as good as there.

"But those have to be sold," Andrula had said in an understanding way.

"Oh, no, they are all for us, and the best ones are for my wife and my daughter!" was his reply. And Kosta's mother had written how much she was looking forward to meeting her new granddaughter. All Andrula had to do now was to learn to say "Father" to Kosta. But she was sure she would manage that, too.

When they finally climbed into the sailboat which was to take them to the next big island where they would board a steamer, Andrula refused to go down into the cabin with her mother. It was very early in the morning and still cold, but she begged for permission to stay on deck. She leaned against the railing of the boat and listened to the rushing of the waves against the keel. They sailed past Ryos and Anti-Ryos and even past Hyria, though at some distance. Slowly the darkness faded to a cold gray. Soon it would be light and she would be able to have a last look at her golden island.

Suddenly, out of the water, came a soft whistle. A voice spoke to her—the voice that she knew so well, that she loved like the voice of her mother.

"Andrula, Andrulitsa!" called the dolphin. "Can you hear me?"

Andrula looked around quickly at the helmsman, but he gave no indication that he had heard anything. She bent lower over the edge of the boat and whispered.

"Yes, yes! I hear you, my dolphin!"

"Are you leaving for good, Andrula?"

"Yes, forever."

"Then you will soon forget us."

"Never!" Andrula cried. "Never. How could I ever forget Hyria and you! Quick, tell me how everyone is on the island!"

"They all send their love, Andrula," answered the dolphin, "especially your little fauns. And I've been asked to tell you they are dancing a Tsamikos now that is a joy to see. Little Battos no longer has a heavy tongue, and so he does not want to be called Battos anymore, but Phaeax, in your honor. Phaeax means 'Radiant Arrival.' Are you listening, Andrula?"

"I am. I hear every word," answered Andrula, and once more she promised: "I will never forget any of you."

"No, because you are faithful, and you drank from Hyria's eternal water," said the dolphin.

With that he turned around and was gone like an arrow.

Just then the sun rose.

Andrula stood for a moment, very still. Then she pushed her scarf back and scanned the sea with sharp eyes. It was all light now. There! Over there he leaped! Three, four, five times the dolphin hurled himself out over the waves, full of power and grace.

His last greeting.

Andrula tore off her scarf and waved it high in the air.

"Joy go with you!" she shouted as loud as she could. "Joy go with you, my dolphin!"

About the Author and Artist

Katherine Allfrey was born in Westphalia, Germany, and attended school there. "I was a solitary child," she says, "and learned to read very early, everything that came my way. For as long as I remember I wanted to travel, an ambition I realized as soon as I was twenty-one and free to do so. I never dreamed of being a writer until I had children and was asked for the stories I heard as a child."

Mrs. Allfrey lived for five years in Athens, where her interest in Greek mythology and history was aroused. *Golden Island,* set in the Greek Islands in the Aegean Sea, was awarded the German Children's Book Prize in 1964, under the title *Delphinensommer*. Mrs. Allfrey and her husband, both citizens of Great Britain, live near Bristol, England.

John Kaufmann, a native New Yorker, studied at the Pennsylvania Academy of Fine Arts, the Art Students League, and the Istituto Statale d'Arte in Florence, Italy. In 1959 he traveled through Europe and spent three months in Greece, at Delphi, Athens, and the islands of Mykonos and Crete. Mr. Kaufmann now lives in Fresh Meadows, New York, with his wife and two young sons.